HEAD OVER HEART

From the Chicken House

To be honest, I'm sometimes still scared of other cultures. When people look different, believe in different things and eat food I've never heard of, I worry they might feel the same about me, and we won't have a good time. But Colette Victor's cool story shows how friends can be really good at making all kinds of differences fit together, even if everything starts out scary – in the end we don't have to be the same to get on really well!

Barry Cunningham
Publisher

HEAD OVER HEART

Colette Victor

Chicken House

2 Palmer Street, Frome, Somerset BA11 1DS

Text © Colette Victor 2014

First published in Great Britain in 2014
The Chicken House
2 Palmer Street
Frome, Somerset, BA11 1DS
United Kingdom
www.doublecluck.com

Cover and interior design by Helen Crawford-White
Cover photograph © Olena Zaskochenko/Shutterstock
Typeset by Dorchester Typesetting Group Ltd
Printed and bound in Great Britain by CPI Group (UK) Ltd, Croydon, CR0 4YY

The paper used in this Chicken House book is made from wood grown in sustainable
forests.

1 3 5 7 9 10 8 6 4 2

British Library Cataloguing in Publication data available.

PB ISBN 978-1-909489-73-8
eISBN 978-1-909489-74-5

For my daughters Juliet and Stella,
Kristen and Jessie

1

I'm lying under the hydrangea bush at the bottom of our garden. My father mowed the lawn this morning and the smell of cut grass makes me think of the lazy summer afternoons to come. The huge leaves hang over me, shielding me from my mum's eyes and the sun. I can just see my old swing and part of the veranda, and the little purple-and-yellow viola in the window box by the kitchen. Even though they're too small to see from here, I know there'll be loads of bees buzzing around them.

I started coming here when I was a little kid and needed a place to hide away. I was playing with a tennis ball indoors one day and I knocked over my mum's favourite vase, the one she got from some aunt when she got married. I was only five, but I knew I was in big trouble, so I ran outside and hid here, under the hydrangea bush. It didn't save me, though – I was still sent to my room to think about what I'd done. I absolutely hated *thinking about what I'd done* when I was five, and I still do. But at least I found this place: my secret corner.

It's where I come when I need to think. Not about simple things like homework or friends or my mum moaning at me – those are for the bus or while I'm doing the chores or something. No, my secret corner is reserved for the important problems. Really, really serious ones.

I tug at a blade of grass. The part that's sheathed inside another layer is a yellowish colour. I nibble at it because I know it will be soft and sweet. And while I'm doing this, I'm thinking. I'm wondering why other people have these peaceful lives that flow along like big, fat easy rivers. *My* life is full of rapids and waterfalls and crocodiles and sharks. And yes, I do know sharks don't actually swim around in rivers, but that's how it feels – like there are these huge obstacles swimming all around me and I have to spend half my life dodging them.

So here's my shark-problem number one.

Today is Kelly's birthday party. Kelly moved here at the start of the school year and she's the first real best friend I've ever had. She's different from the other girls. She's smart, she says what she thinks and she's not into make-up and things like that. She's more interested in things that really matter, like not being a hypocrite and standing up to bullies. She's skinny, like me, but her hair's blonde and she wears it in a ponytail. Anyway, she's invited the whole class to a barbecue in the park. Of course, she expects me to be there and I really, really want to go. I can't *not* go.

But at the same time, and I mean at *exactly* the same

time – not yesterday, not last week, not tomorrow, but *today* – I'm expected to go shopping with my mum and all my female relatives to buy a dress for my cousin's wedding.

Which brings me to shark-problem number two: my mum wants to buy me a headscarf.

The thing is, I honestly have no idea if I want to wear one or not. I've never even thought about it. But yesterday I got my period for the first time, which kind of officially makes me a *woman* – in my mum's eyes at least. When I told her she screamed and hugged me, and then ran off to phone everyone in her address book. I couldn't believe she did that – I practically fainted with embarrassment. It was like I'd won the Nobel Prize and swum the English Channel all in one day: my mum had turned biology into personal achievement. Meantime it was just my body going from one phase to the next.

When she finally managed to tear her ear away from the phone, she remembered me sitting all by myself on the veranda. She came outside and offered me a glass of tea.

'When we go shopping tomorrow,' she said, 'I'd like to . . . you can choose a . . . your first headscarf . . .'

See what I mean about waterfalls and rapids and crocodiles and sharks?

I drop my chewed blade of grass and pull out a new one. I sigh as I pop it into my mouth. I have absolutely no idea what I'm going to do.

Weddings are a really big deal with us. I mean a really,

really big deal. OK, I know they're a big deal in all cultures but the bigness of this deal overshadows all others and makes them look pretty lame. I've been to weddings where there were over a thousand guests – as if anyone actually *knows* a thousand people. Basically, if you've ever passed someone on the street – not necessarily on the same side of the street – you're entitled to show up at their wedding.

Families save up for years for them. They don't go on holiday, they drive around in beat-up old cars and take out loans from the bank. And what do they spend this money on? Rented limousines, lavish dishes, dresses that shimmer and glitter with diamanté. And it's not only the bride that has to shimmer and glitter. No, it's the entire family. Now, I'm not big on glittering and shimmering, and I'm definitely not big on shopping trips with an endless row of aunts and cousins, but even I know there's no way I can turn up at a family wedding in my favourite jeans. For starters, my mum would probably have a heart attack on the spot.

I've known about Kelly's barbecue for ages but I didn't bother telling my parents about it. The shopping trip was already planned. It would be like going up to my mum and telling her I wanted to stay home and swat flies instead of going shopping – in her world, a friend's birthday party is just not important.

But I can't be the only one in the class who doesn't show up. Especially since I'm her best friend. What will I say to her on Monday? *Sorry, I had to go shopping?* She'll never understand.

'Zeyneb? Where are you?'

I peep out from beneath the hydrangea leaves. My mum's standing on the veranda, wringing the dishcloth she always carries. She's wearing her ancient green apron with little white flowers over an ankle-length, dark-blue dress. She's got on black stockings, these disgusting butch shoes (practical, she calls them) and a beige headscarf with brown flowers covering her hair. Honestly, who still wears beige?

'Zeyne-e-e-b.' It's amazing how many syllables she can make out of my name.

'Coming, *Anne*.' I sigh and crawl out from underneath my shrub. (*Anne* is our word for 'mum'. But don't pronounce it *Anne*, like the girl's name. No, you're supposed to say the *e* at the end, the same *e* you hear in 'egg'.)

'What exactly do you do out there under those plants all day long?' she says, as I slowly make my way across the garden.

I drop my head to roll my eyes – I know if she sees me do it, I'll get an ear-bashing.

'And I said we were leaving thirty minutes ago, didn't I? Just look at you!' She plucks grass off my T-shirt.

I push her hand away. '*Anne*, stop it.'

'You're just like your father,' she goes on. 'Can't come inside without bringing half the garden with you. Now get upstairs and put on something decent. We have to be at your aunt's house in ten minutes.'

5

'But *Anne*, I don't want . . .' I stop. I just don't know how to say this. *I don't want to go.*

Without warning, she stretches out one hand and strokes my cheek. Her stern brown eyes soften. 'Today is a big day, *kizim*,' she says. *Kizim* – my girl. 'We're going to buy your first headscarf, remember?'

'But *Anne*—' I try again, chewing my bottom lip.

'You have to grow up some time, my girl, even your body is telling you that.' Her hands make a sweeping gesture to take in my frame. 'This is not a little girl standing in front of me any more. This is a young woman.'

'*Anne*, please—'

'And I think your cousin's wedding would be a good place to wear your first headscarf.'

Her cheeks are all shiny, her eyes glistening. I don't know if I've ever seen her look this happy before.

'I'm not even sure if . . .' I stop. Her mouth drops and her eyes meet mine – they're almost pleading. 'I . . . I haven't made up my mind yet,' I say.

'I'm sure you know it's the right thing for a good Muslim girl to do?' She pulls back her hand from my cheek and starts wringing the dishcloth again.

I nod, even though I don't agree with her. I know loads of good Muslim girls who don't wear headscarves and loads of hypocrites who do. I'd like to tell her that – but of course I don't.

My mum sighs at my silence. 'Zeyneb, you're a smart girl and I can see you've been thinking about this. I just thought . . . it would be nice if you chose a pretty scarf today.'

It's right then that an image flits into my head: Kelly's present lying wrapped up, hidden in the corner of my cupboard – the new book by that writer she's into. I bought it with the money I got for *Bayram*, the sugar festival to celebrate the end of our month of fasting.

What am I going to do? I realize I'm going to have to lie to someone.

My phone saves me. That funky new ringtone I downloaded last night sounds from the pocket of my jeans. I take it out and look at it.

It's a text from Kelly, and even though there are only three words, they're enough to make my heart practically jump out of my throat: **Alex is coming!**

Alex . . . OMG!

And that's shark-problem number three . . .

'Zeyneb!' my mum says crossly. 'Put that thing away when I'm speaking to you.'

I look up at her. Treat your parents politely and gently – that's what I've been taught. And Kelly's text has helped me make up my mind. But I can't lie to *Anne*.

I find my father kneeling on a half-empty bag of compost in the garden shed, fussing with two trays of seedlings. There's a small brown leaf clinging to his hair, mud on his shoes, twigs stuck to his pullover, and a ladybird crawling along his shoulder. Like *Anne* says, he never comes inside without bringing a little piece of outside with him. He goes to work in the car factory every day, but deep down he's a gardener. When he gets home, he shovels down a piece of my mum's *pide* – flat Turkish bread – drinks a glass of tea, and goes right out the door again and off to his allotment.

If I don't have too much homework, I go with him. I jump on my bike and ride slowly next to him while his long, patient strides carry him down the road. I chatter away, telling him about things that happened to me at school. He doesn't say anything, just keeps on walking – but later on, when we're kneeling next to the aubergines, our fingernails black with soil, he'll say something to me in that quiet way of his that lets me know he was listening to every word.

Now, in the shed, he says, 'Did you talk to Mrs Berger yet? Did you tell her how that boy spoke to you? You know it works two ways, don't you? A boy needs to respect a girl too.'

Biting my bottom lip, I nod. I half wish I hadn't said anything to him about the stupid remark David made to me in class. Things aren't always as simple as he thinks they are, though I often wish they were.

He carries on: 'It's not just book knowledge you learn at school, *kizim* . . .'

'I know, I know, *Baba*.' I smile because I know what's coming.

'It's the ways of the world. The way they do things in this country.' He's always saying things like that, my dad. He sits back on his haunches and looks up at me. 'I got these from Ali down at the allotment,' he says, holding up a seedling in a pot. 'Some kind of yellow chilli we don't get here.'

I want to look at the yellow chilli but all I can think about is Kelly's present and her text. I gather my courage in both hands. I'm not going to let her down.

'*Baba*, I need to talk to you,' I say.

'What is it?'

'I can't go shopping for a dress with *Anne*.' There, I've said it.

Baba frowns and his knees slip off the bag of compost. He puts one hand on the ground to keep his balance. 'Come on, Zeyneb. This trip has been planned for a long time.'

'No, seriously, I can't go – and I've got a very good reason.'

My dad gets to his feet and takes my right hand in both of his. The dark, wet soil rubs off on my own fingers. '*Kizim*, we all have to do things we don't want to. It's called growing up. Besides, this afternoon means a lot to your mum.'

'But *Baba*, I have a French test tomorrow.'

'A French test? And you've only found out about this now?'

'Kelly texted me a few minutes ago. She asked me to go over there and learn with her. Otherwise I would've completely forgotten about it. You want to see the text?' It's a risk, but I know my dad would never dream of reading my messages.

He shakes his head and lets go of my hand, then bends down and starts fussing with his seedlings again. He's thinking.

'It's a really big test, *Baba*,' I carry on shamelessly. 'It counts for fifty per cent of our end-of-year marks. It's on the . . . um . . . conjugation of verbs.'

'Can't you learn for it later?' he says, carefully re-potting another seedling. 'You can catch a bus home and study as soon as you've chosen a dress . . .'

'I need more time, *Baba*. Otherwise I'm going to fail.'

He sighs a great big sigh, as if he's trying to blow out all the distress I'm causing him. 'All right. Get your books and go over to Kelly's. I'll speak to your mum.'

Yes! I knew it would be easier with Baba.

I want to throw my arms around him and plant a fat kiss on his forehead – but that would be way over the top for a French test, so I flash him a smile instead. 'Thank you, *Baba*.'

'You're going to have to make this up to your mum, you know?'

'I know,' I say over my shoulder as I practically skip towards the house. 'She can choose a dress for me. Something blue.'

'Go and speak to her yourself, Zeyneb,' he calls after me sternly, but I pretend not to hear.

Up in my bedroom, as I grab Kelly's present from my cupboard, I let my hair down from its ponytail and give it a good shake. Taking my mascara from its hiding place in a drawer, I shove it into my jeans pocket.

I've got away with it. Even though something in me wishes I hadn't.

But I ignore the feeling, pushing it deep down out of reach, and text Kelly: B there in 10.

2

I'm in the park opposite Kelly's apartment block – that's where the barbecue is. I pedalled my legs off for ten whole minutes to get here on time and help Kelly set up. Her mum was here for a while, but then she went back to the flat. She said she was sure we wouldn't want a grown-up hanging around. How cool is that! It's just us now.

The park is big, with a kind of dip in the middle and a play area for little kids where Kelly and I hardly ever go. We like the spot where we are now, by two old chestnut trees. Their branches stretch out like huge protective arms and there's a bench beneath one of them. That's where Kelly and I usually sit when I visit her. We always want to be outside, even when it's cold. I'm like my dad that way. We've sat on that bench for hours, teasing each other, laughing, moaning about our lives. That's where I told her about my feelings for Alex. Feelings I'm not supposed to have. I don't think she quite gets it, though – she thinks everyone can simply feel whatever they like.

Everything's ready for the barbecue and we're just waiting for everyone to turn up. There are two long plastic tables with garden chairs arranged around them, and they're laid with colourful paper plates, plastic knives and forks, serviettes and paper cups. With the sun shining like this, the tables nestled in the shade under the trees, some of their white blossoms scattered in the longish grass, this has got to be the best place in the whole city. Or even the whole world! I wouldn't want to be anywhere else.

At the same time, I know it's the one place I shouldn't be. The one place my parents would never expect me to be. *Just forget about them and enjoy the party!* I tell myself. But somehow I can't.

'It looks lovely,' I say to Kelly.

'And Alex? Do you think *he'll* like it?' she asks, giggling and flashing me a knowing look.

Why'd she have to go and say something like that when I'm already feeling guilty? I give her upper arm a firm twist.

'Hey!' She laughs, jumping away and swatting at me, which makes me laugh too.

A little way off are two barbecues, each with a neat pile of charcoal just waiting to be lit. When I was little, my mum made me promise I'd be very, *very* careful about eating meat at non-Muslims' houses. 'Just tell them you're a vegetarian,' she said, when I went to Kelly's house for the first time.

But Kelly's mum, Annelies, wasn't having any of it. 'I'd never dream of giving Zeyneb pork,' she'd said when *Anne* came to pick me up (or rather, nose around to make sure my new best friend wasn't going to lead me down the path to hell).

'I wouldn't expect you to go to any trouble,' my mum had muttered, but there was no way she could squirm out of it without being rude, so, with tight lips, she'd agreed. From that day on I was allowed to eat meat at Kelly's house. Only at Kelly's house, mind you. Everywhere else I still had to say I was vegetarian. Honestly, I've eaten enough potatoes and vegetables to last me a lifetime.

And so that's why there are two barbecues: a Muslim one and a non-Muslim one. Some people think it's a bit extreme, but it's the way I've been raised – and anyway, loads of people won't eat frogs' legs or snails and no one calls them extreme. At least I'm keeping *that* promise to my mum, I think. But that just makes me feel guilty all over again and I wonder if my mum's found me a dress yet . . . *No, I'm not going to think about that.*

Enjoy yourself, Zeyneb. You wanted to be here.

'Shall I try to light the fire?' I say to change the subject. 'Or shall we wait and ask one of the boys?'

'Anything a boy can do, a girl can do better,' Kelly bites back. It's like her personal motto. I sometimes wish it could be mine too.

'The lighter's over there in that basket.'

Twenty minutes later, both piles of charcoal are being licked by limp flames and I'm trying to fan more life into them with the lid of a cool-box. Some of the others have started arriving – David, Julie, Christine and . . .

'Zeyneb!' Kelly whispers urgently behind me. 'He's here.'

14

I know exactly who she means. In a panic I spin round to face her. Kelly stares at me, her eyes huge.

'Oh, no . . .' she gasps. Her hand, holding a plastic cup of Fanta, freezes halfway to her lips.

'What's wrong?' I ask, glancing wildly around. *Where is he? What do I do now?*

'Zeyneb,' Kelly splutters, 'your face!'

'What about my face?'

'You've got charcoal all over it. Wash it off!'

'How'm I supposed to wash it off?' I'm in total panic mode now. 'There's no water anywhere.'

As Kelly makes a dash to the basket of supplies I start rubbing my face, then realize . . . my hands are black as well! I bend down and wipe my fingers on the grass. Kelly's back, holding a paper serviette and a bottle of sparkling water.

'Try this.' She's grinning at me and I can sort of see why.

'Thanks,' I say but I can see her attention isn't on me any more. It's on something beyond my right shoulder.

'Hi, Kelly.' I hear his voice behind me. 'Hi, Zeyneb . . .'

I don't dare turn round. 'Hi, Alex,' I say, trying to sound casual but achieving the exact opposite. Kelly's wiped the grin off her face, but her eyes are sparkling.

'Happy birthday,' he says.

'Thanks,' I reply, and that does it for Kelly.

'I think he means me, dork!'

Now she's really laughing, and so is he.

I could just melt into the ground with embarrassment.

It's even worse than yesterday, when *Anne* phoned the whole world to tell them about my first period. I feel my face getting hot from my neck up and I shut my eyes. Maybe if I keep them closed, Alex will go away and come back later and we can start over?

No chance. Time to be brave.

I turn to face him, ready to say something in my defence, but I have to catch my breath as my eyes fall on That Face: jet-black hair with a fringe flopping over his left eye . . . a dimple in his right cheek . . . smooth olive skin . . . a wide grin . . . eyes crinkling at the sides . . . He looks so sure of himself. I hate that about him but, at the same time, I love it. He's laughing at me. For the second time in less than a minute.

My mouth is open, trying to speak, but nothing will come out. I'm overcome by Awe and Wonder. The same Awe and Wonder that's been overcoming me the last couple of weeks each time I look at That Face. Don't know why it happened. Don't even know when exactly. I mean, he's been in my class for the last two years and I'd never noticed him before. At least not in this way. So why now? Kelly says it's called falling in love. I don't dare call it anything. I'm *Baba* and *Anne*'s daughter, a good Muslim girl. I know perfectly well how dangerous a word like *love* can be.

'Didn't anyone tell you, Zeyneb,' he says, leaning in, 'mascara's meant to go on your eyes, not your whole face?'

I have no comeback. All I can do is stare, my mouth gaping like a goldfish's.

But Kelly's got my back. Her arm shoots out and she playfully punches him on the shoulder. 'The least you can do is help!' she says, winking at me.

'Ow!' he complains. 'That really hurt.'

The spell's broken and I'm walking away with long, determined strides, the serviette and bottle of water in my hands. Kelly's bossing Alex around, telling him to take care of the fire, giving me a chance to get away. Behind the chestnut trees, I wet the serviette and start rubbing away at my cheeks. Rubbing, and rubbing some more, until the serviette's completely black and crumbled into a hundred pieces.

Celeste, one of the kindest girls in my class, is suddenly next to me. 'Here we go,' she says. Like an angel sent down to earth, she's holding out a small hand-mirror and a plastic container of wet-wipes. 'Kelly sent me to check on you.'

'Thanks,' I gasp gratefully and return to my frenzied face-cleaning. Once I've checked myself in the mirror and Celeste has assured me ten times that every last bit of charcoal has gone, I allow myself to be led back to the party.

Both barbecues are roaring now and everyone's arrived. Kelly is pretending to be delighted as she unwraps a fancy bottle of bath foam. I smile because I know how much she hates all that girlie stuff. I quietly join the crowd that's gathered round my best friend and slip my own small, rectangular present on to the table in front of her.

Kelly's eyes find mine. 'Is that . . . ?'

I nod.

'The new one?'

I nod again.

'Thanks, Zey, I can't wait to read it.'

Jamal produces a football and challenges the girls to a match against the boys. Hardly fair, I think, given all the hours of practice the boys get during break, but I don't say anything. Kelly, who's into any kind of sports, grabs the ball from him and kicks it in the direction of the open grass. Everyone goes charging after it.

Everyone except Alex, it would seem. 'Maybe I should give you barbecue lessons?' he says. He's grinning at me again, dimple and all, and the Awe and Wonder are right back where they were ten minutes ago. Words are gone. But no! I don't want to go back to my gaping goldfish act. I want to have fun, I want to enjoy the party. I didn't go to all that trouble of lying to my parents for nothing. I want to talk to Alex.

I force myself to say something – anything: 'I like looking like a coal miner.'

What! Has anyone ever said something so lame before in the history of the universe?

'Takes a lot of talent to perfect a look like that,' I go on, even though a voice in my head is saying, *Shut up, Zeyneb! Shut up now!*

But something incredible happens: Alex laughs – and this time he's laughing with me, not at me. I think. And then, even better – or worse, I can't tell which – he leans sideways and nudges my shoulder with his own. Our bodies actually touch! My insides are toffee again but, at the same time, I know now I'll get through this afternoon, not just freeze up when he talks to me. In fact, I'm looking forward to it.

'C'mon, you going to join in the game?' I ask, gesturing to where the others are marking out goal posts with big stones.

'I'm not much of a footballer.' Alex shrugs.

'You're just scared the girls will win,' I say, taking off towards the makeshift pitch.

'In your dreams,' he laughs, and speeds past me.

We're all gathered around the table where Kelly is about to cut her chocolate birthday cake. She's texted her mum to come and have some with us and I'm looking in that direction to see if I can spot Annelies.

That's when I see him. My father. Standing there between the parked cars. He's a tall man so it's hard to miss him.

He's not supposed to be here, not supposed to be here *at all*! And yet he's standing right there, next to our family car at the edge of the park, his arms crossed. Watching us.

In panic I turn my head away. I stare, instead, at Kelly's shoulders with her little spaghetti straps. My body is suddenly covered in a thin layer of ice-cold sweat.

3

'Oh, no!' I mutter.

Kelly looks at me. She can see something's wrong. Her face is full of questions but I turn away from her. She's not important right now. I feel sick. I can hardly breathe.

'Your dad,' Kelly says, pointing her chin in his direction.

'I know,' I answer. It feels like I've been punched in the stomach.

'Why is he here? Didn't you come on your bike?'

'I did,' I say softly.

I step away from the table and start moving slowly towards my father. My eyes are fixed on him, trying to lock on to his eyes, so I can read what's there. Underneath his thick black moustache his lips are pressed together. As soon as he sees me looking at him he turns his head away. In disgust. I realize that immediately.

Kelly calls after me, 'What's going on?'

'I'm in big trouble,' is all I can say. I'm not sure if she hears me.

'Zeyneb?'

But I don't turn round. I don't explain, don't say goodbye to anyone. I have to reach my father as quickly as I can to start putting things right.

'*Baba*,' I call, rushing towards him.

Still not looking at me, he opens the back door of the car.

'*Baba*?' I try again.

He waits, his back turned to me as he stares over the roofs of the cars. It's as if he hasn't even heard my voice. My thousand-and-one apologies and explanations are stuck in my throat and he's not going to give me a chance to let them out.

I cast my eyes down at the cracked tarmac and climb into the back seat.

He shuts the door quietly. My fear evaporates and instead I feel *angry*. Why can't he just slam it? Why won't he yell at me? Why does he have to be so calm?

He gets into the driver's seat and starts the car.

I've never known the five-minute drive home to take so long. I can hear my heart beating, and my breathing is fast and shallow. All I can do is stare at his broad, unmovable shoulders and black head of hair. At last he pulls into the drive, gets out and walks into the house without once acknowledging me. Desperately, I follow him inside.

To get to the staircase, I have to walk through the lounge. My mum's on the sofa. I see her eyes fly up to mine, full of questions. 'Why?' I read in them. But her lips say nothing. Next to her is *Teyze* – aunty – my mum's older sister. She's adjusting her dark-blue headscarf with one hand while holding my mum's hand with the other, as if there's just been a death in the family or something. She's stern and skinny and likes to think she's perfect – she doesn't bother looking at me. My eleven-year-old cousin Semra is attached to her side, as always. My five-year-old nephew, Silvan, and two-year-old niece, Dilara, are fighting over a fire engine on the carpet.

'Zeyneb!' Silvan squeals when he sees me. He and Dilara immediately abandon the fire engine and jump to their feet.

Elif, my sister, walks in from the kitchen carrying a tray with a teapot and glasses. 'Sit down, you two,' she says.

'But I want to play with Ze-e-e-eyneb,' Dilara wails.

'Sit down, I said.'

Without a word, Silvan and Dilara sit back down on the carpet, their little eyes fixed on me.

Elif looks at me. Her eyes crinkle up in sympathy. I give her a little nod, bite my bottom lip and cross the lounge to the stairs.

Finally I reach my bedroom and throw myself down on my bed. Feeling my phone poke me in the pelvis, I turn on my back and retrieve it from my pocket. The screen is blank. The battery must've run out. Oh, no, that means . . .

I rush over to my dressing table and plug the phone into the charger, then I punch in the password.

There are eight missed calls and texts.

One from my mum.

Four from my father.

Two from Elif.

The last one from Kelly: **Alex asked 4 ur number.**

Even though I saved for months for this phone, even though it's my most prized possession, today I hate it. Look at how much trouble I'm in because of a stupid flat battery. And that's nothing compared to how much more trouble I'll be in if my parents find out Alex has my number. I hope Kelly didn't give it to him. No, I hope she did. Oh, I don't know . . .

Now I'm crying. Huge, loud, racking sobs. Just like a baby, but I don't care. This afternoon I was convinced that this was the best day of my whole life. Now it's turning out to be the worst. All because of this phone! I fling it against the wall and watch it smash into pieces.

I'm still on my bed. It's been hours and no one's come to my room yet. I'm listening to the sounds of my family going about their business. My mum calls everyone for supper (except me, of course). I'm starving. I hardly ate anything at the barbecue this afternoon. I was far too busy concentrating on where Alex was, what he was doing, when he was coming closer, to even think about eating. Downstairs I hear the clinking of cutlery on plates and, every now and then, the low murmur of voices. I'm hoping Elif will knock on my door with a plate of food in her hands and, more importantly, an explanation. What went wrong? How was I caught out? Why did my dad go to Kelly's?

But the knock doesn't come. I hear my mum say good-bye to Elif and the little ones, and then her car starts up and she drives off.

The truth is, though, I don't need an explanation. I can put two and two together and figure it out for myself. It goes like this:

My mum phones me for my approval of some dress or other she wants to buy. I don't answer. She phones my father and he tries to phone me. I don't answer. He phones again. No answer. Four times. (The rule in our house is I always leave my phone on and answer it the minute they call.) Believing I've been knocked off my bike by a bus or something, he climbs into his car and drives over to Kelly's house. He sees us in the park. He knows I've lied to him. The details of the lie don't interest him. Who knows how long he stands there, watching us, waiting for me. Probably the whole time, for all I know.

Why doesn't he come into my room and shout at me? If not him, then at least my mum? How can she pass up an opportunity like this? Where she's 100 per cent right and I have no leg to stand on. Isn't having a go at me her favourite hobby?

Jumping up from my bed, I stomp over to my window and pinch off the dead flowers on the African violets on my windowsill. It's not fair to put this on my parents. The person I'm really cross with is myself. And I should be. I'm stern with myself, as if that will somehow save me. But what does it change? How will my anger at myself fix anything? Especially if there's a tiny part of me that still isn't sorry, even now. A part of me that's glad I went to the barbecue, glad I talked to Alex. I wouldn't take it back if I could. Try as hard as I can, I can't keep that part of me quiet. And even if I could, how is it going to make my father speak to me again?

I'm back on my bed, staring at a fly buzzing round the ceiling. Beyond my door I hear the getting-ready-for-bed sounds. And then the house is silent. My eyes are heavy. I try to fight off sleep. I pull the duvet over me and wait for the familiar sound of my father's footsteps. Surely he won't skip his ritual of planting a kiss on my forehead before he goes to bed? He can't be that cross with me, can he? I lie awake for ages, and the sound of the floorboards not creaking under my father's weight screams at me. I never knew silence could be this loud.

I'm drifting on the edge of sleep when, at last, I hear my door open. I peer out from beneath my duvet. A shaft of soft, orange light from the passage falls into my bedroom and I see my father's face looking in. Quickly I pinch my eyes shut. When I open them his head disappears and the door is closed. No kiss on my forehead tonight.

4

In the morning I'm absolutely starving. I haven't eaten a thing since Kelly's barbecue yesterday afternoon and the smell of fresh, warm bread wafting from our kitchen makes my mouth water.

'Good morning, *Baba*. Good morning, *Anne*,' I say, walking into the kitchen.

My parents stand up from the table. No greeting. They don't even look at me. Nothing. If it wasn't for my place set at the table, I'd think they'd completely forgotten about my existence in the space of one short night.

My mother gives my father a kiss on the cheek. '*Güle güle*,' she says. *Go well*.

Now it's his turn to walk round the table and wait by my chair so I can lean up and give him a kiss, the traditional way we greet our fathers. But he doesn't. He heads for the front door instead.

Taking a sip of tea, I stare at my plate, tears stinging my eyes: a triangle of fresh *pide* bread, a few slices of tomato, some white cheese, a fried pepper and a boiled egg – this is the breakfast we usually get at the weekend. My mum must be feeling bad that I didn't eat anything last night. She's convinced that the skipping of a single meal will lead to instantaneous death by starvation. Maybe if I don't eat, she'll be forced to talk to me. Pushing back first my tears and then my plate, I hear the faintest of gasps escape her lips. But she stays strong and says nothing.

Fifteen minutes later I'm dressed and ready for school. I walk into the kitchen and see her standing with her back to me, staring out of the window. My plate has been cleared and my school lunchbox is sitting on the table.

'Goodbye, *Anne*,' I say, as I always do. 'Have a nice day.'

She doesn't budge.

I must admit it stings far more than I would've imagined. Yesterday the idea of my mum not moaning at me would've sounded like a dream. And even though I know they can't actually ignore me for the rest of my life, even though I know I'm supposed to think they're doing this because they love me, it doesn't soften it.

I wonder what she's put in my lunchbox today. Probably something extra yummy like *lahmacun*, Turkish pizza, to make up for the meals I haven't had. Next to it is my favourite Capri-Sun, Apple-Cherry.

'Have it your way, then,' I mumble – but very quietly so she can't hear my words.

I leave my lunchbox and the drink behind on the table.

On my bike, cycling to school, I'm thinking so hard about how I can make all of this right that I'm not paying attention and a car almost bashes into me at the round-about. It screeches to a stop and the woman inside sounds her horn. She's mad, mouthing angry words at me. I shrug and carry on pedalling. I bet *Anne* and *Baba* would be sorry if I died in a car accident. I bet they'd wish for the rest of their lives they'd spoken to me this morning at breakfast. All because of their stupid shopping trip.

I remember the time when my sister still lived at home and my parents stopped speaking to her. This not-talking-to-their-daughters is their favourite punishment. She was eighteen and my parents found out she had a boyfriend. One of our stupid cousins had seen Elif in town, holding hands with him, and she'd almost broken her neck in her gleeful rush to phone my mum and bust my sister.

I can just imagine the conversation: '*Teyze*, I hate to be the bringer of bad news, but you know what I saw in the shopping centre this afternoon . . .'

That's how it is. Everyone loves to see someone else fall on their face.

It wasn't actually the fact that she had a boyfriend that upset my parents. It's pretty common for us to get married young. I mean, compared to women who aren't Muslim. It was the fact that she was doing it behind their backs. They didn't know the boy, didn't know his family and all that. Plus there was the fact that everyone would gossip. Shameful, they'd call it, and if there's one thing we try to avoid at all costs, it's bringing shame on the family.

I was eight years old when it happened and I was so

confused because, until that moment, I hadn't realized our family could be unhappy. For almost two weeks they said nothing to Elif and she spent most of that time lying on her bed, just sobbing and sobbing. I would sneak into her room, sit at the top of her bed and stroke her hair.

'Just say you're sorry,' was my naive advice to her at the time.

'You know what I'm going to do?' she said one afternoon.

I shook my head.

'I'm going to go live with *Teyze* Havva.' Her voice was full of conviction.

'*Teyze* Havva?' I said. '*Teyze* Havva!'

Our mystery aunt. My mum's eldest sister. The one who ran away years ago, and married a non-Muslim. We'd never met her but we did receive birthday cards from her every year and envelopes with money for *Bayram*. When you're eight it's hard to believe someone you've never met is an actual person. Definitely not a real person who could take in your unhappy sister and let her live with her. My jaw was practically hanging on the bed.

Elif nodded.

'But where . . .' I was totally dumbfounded. 'How do you know where she lives?

'I found her address in that old notebook of *Anne*'s. You know, that one she keeps hidden in her top drawer?'

I nodded. I knew exactly which notebook she was talking about. I'd seen it too when I was snooping in my mum's things, fingering her hand-embroidered handkerchiefs, rubbing her silk headscarves against my cheek.

'What about me?' I'd asked.

'I'll write to you. You can come visit me when you're older . . .'

In the end she didn't run off to live with our mystery aunt. Instead, the boy's parents came to our house to meet *Baba* and *Anne,* and pretty soon after that, Elif and Deniz got engaged. Then there was the wedding, and about nine months later Silvan popped into this world. It all worked out fine. If you don't count the fact that Elif never went on to study nursing like she'd always wanted.

Kelly is waiting for me at the bicycle shed when I arrive at school. Her eyes are nearly popping out of her head. 'Why aren't you answering your phone? What's going on?'

For some reason I don't feel like seeing her, talking to her. 'It's broken,' I mutter as I park my bike next to hers.

'What! What happened?'

'It's broken, that's all. It's no big deal.' I start walking away from her.

'Hey, wait a minute.' Her hand is on my arm and her voice has turned all strict. Her mum probably speaks to her this way when she's moaning at her. 'Your dad shows up at the park to pick you up from my birthday party and your face goes all white. You don't answer my texts and phone calls all night, and now you're telling me the phone you spent six months saving up for is broken and it's no big deal. What's going on?'

'Let go, Kelly. It's none of your business,' I snap and pull away.

'None of my business? Since when—'

I spin round. 'Since you have no idea what it's like to live in a family like mine. Since you have this perfect life with just you and your mum and all your easy little rules. Since you don't know what it's like to have a *real* family.'

Kelly's mouth is hanging open and her eyes are wide. Even while I'm saying these words a part of my brain is screaming, *Shut up, Zeyneb!* But another part just doesn't care and that part is stronger. I want to hurt Kelly and I don't know why. Yes, I do – it's because she doesn't have to choose.

Doesn't have to choose between shopping with her mum and her best friend's party.

Doesn't have to choose between wearing a headscarf and disappointing her family.

Doesn't have to choose between being a good Muslim girl and sneaking around behind her parents' backs.

And right now, right this very second, I hate her for that. I really and truly hate her. Even though she's standing there with her gaping mouth and tears welling up in her eyes.

I know I've hurt her and that I'm going to be sorry later. I already feel it surging up somewhere inside, but it doesn't stop me. I carry right on hating her.

Turning away, I stomp off to line up.

5

The horrible school day is finally behind me – not talking to Kelly and trying to avoid Alex because it's just too complicated to deal with right now. I jump on my bike and pedal away as fast as I can. I know where I'm going, and it's not home.

At number 64, I chuck my bike down on the lawn and charge up to the front door. The day shoes that usually sit in a neat little row outside the door are gone and in their place are four pairs of slippers. So, they're not home. I knock all the same. I wait.

Nothing.

Plonking myself down on the top step, I wonder where they can be. I stare out at their messy garden and make a list, like *Baba* would do: grass too long, weeds all over the beds, shrubs that need pruning and not a flower in sight . . . If I wasn't feeling so depressed, I might've gone to the shed to fetch shears. My empty stomach is groaning. I'm actually light-headed from hunger. Leaning back on my rucksack while the sun bakes down on my legs, I try to focus my attention on something else.

I'm startled by the sound of a child shrieking, 'Zeyneb!'

Sitting up, I realize I must've fallen asleep. As I rub my eyes, my niece and nephew clamber out of the family car in the driveway and rush to throw themselves at me in delight. Elif is battling with bags of shopping, her oversized handbag and a little rucksack shaped like a train. I get up to help her.

'What are you doing here?' she asks.

I shrug.

I've got one of the shopping bags in my hand and I scratch around in it to find something to eat. Pulling open a plastic packet, I pop two cherry tomatoes into my mouth. The seeds shoot out as I bite down on them.

'Zeyneb,' Elif says in disgust, 'you haven't even washed them.'

I sigh. 'It's an emergency.'

'Come on,' she says. 'Let's go in and talk about it.'

I help the kids out of their day shoes and into their slippers. I put on a pair of guest slip-ons myself and follow my sister into the house.

We get the two little ones settled at the kitchen table, each with a chocolate-spread sandwich and a glass of milk. Elif and I are unpacking the groceries. We don't say much. Our movements are perfectly synchronized through years of repetition. (One of my mum's favourite orders is: 'I want you to go over to your sister and help her out for a couple of hours. She's got her hands full with those two little ones.') My eyes are fixed on Dilara: each time she tears off a crust, I'm at her side to pick it off her plate and shove it into my mouth. We get everything into the cupboards and Elif takes out the chopping board and a couple of onions.

'Is there anything I can do?' I ask.

'Yes, take out the bread and make yourself a sandwich before you start eating my children,' Elif says, pulling a face at me.

'Which one should I eat first?'

Elif and I laugh while the children stare at us with puzzled little faces. I lean over to ruffle their hair and they scamper off to play.

A few minutes later, I'm sitting opposite my sister, climbing into my pile of sandwiches – white bread topped with slices of the sticky preserved figs my mum made last summer. And a glass of orange juice.

'I've been trying to get hold of you since last night. Why don't you answer your phone?' she asks.

'It's broken.'

'What do you mean, broken?'

'Don't lecture me, Elif. It's broken, that's all.'

'So how does *Anne* know you're here?'

I shrug.

'What!'

'I don't have a phone. How am I supposed to let her know? Besides, she's still not talking to . . .'

'That's no excuse, Zeyneb. You know you have to let her know where you are. Aren't you in enough trouble already?' Elif grabs her handbag and rummages around for her phone. Pushing it across the counter towards me, she says, 'Call her.'

I don't move.

'Call her,' she repeats, her voice stern.

I glare at her. 'Whose side are you on anyway?'

'Since when are there sides in this family? She must be frantic. She probably thinks you've been knocked down or something.'

'Good. That will teach her to—'

'Stop being such a child.' She pushes the phone into my hand.

She's already punched in my mum's number and the phone is dialling. I put it down on the counter and stare decisively out of the window.

Sighing heavily, she picks the thing up again and speaks into it. '*Anne*? She's here with me.' Listening to my mum's voice, she nods. 'Fine. Don't worry. Everything's fine.' She rolls her eyes. 'Yes, yes, I've given her something to eat.'

For the longest time we don't discuss what happened yesterday. While Elif prepares the supper, I go outside with Silvan and Dilara and start weeding one of the flower beds. I always feel better when my hands are in the soil. My brother-in-law, Deniz, arrives home from work. He's not exactly my favourite person in the whole world, but I greet him politely. Secretly I think Elif deserves a better husband, someone who realizes how special she is

35

and doesn't take her for granted. He nods curtly. Being both a child (in his eyes, at least) and a girl, I don't warrant much more than the briefest acknowledgement. When supper is ready, we all sit down at the table to eat. My hunger still hasn't vanished completely, even after the pile of sandwiches I ate. I gobble down two portions of Elif's meatballs, *bulgur pilaf* (similar to rice, only better) and *cacık* – diluted yogurt mixed with minced cucumbers. After popping the little ones in the bath, Elif and I get them into bed and they fall asleep.

Then we sit in the kitchen, our small glasses of red *çay*, Turkish tea, in front of us. Hot and sweet, as always.

'Can I stay here tonight?' I start, but I already know the answer. Even if I manage to convince my sister, Deniz will never buy it. As it is, I know he's irritated that I'm here. He thinks his wife's attention, once the kids are in bed, should be for him alone.

'Don't be silly,' she says. 'You're just making it worse by avoiding them.'

'*I'm* avoiding *them*? That's a joke,' I scoff.

'Don't be so stubborn, Zeyneb. Go home, kiss *Baba*'s hand, tell them you're sorry and everything will go back to normal.'

I roll my eyes at her.

She carries on. '*Anne* bought you a lovely dress yesterday for the wedding. She's dying to show it to you. To see you try it on.'

I groan at the thought of the huge shimmering, bejewelled mass I'll have to prance around in. I can just picture it. She has the most terrible taste. Last year at a cousin's circumcision celebration, she wore a dress that looked like it had come straight out of the Cinderella movie.

'It's sky-blue. Really pretty. She did her best to find the simplest one there was,' Elif explains.

Instead of asking for more details, like she's hoping, I roll my eyes again.

'There's just the tiniest bit of lace round the bust. You hardly notice it at all . . .'

Our conversation is interrupted by Deniz coming into the kitchen. 'I'm going to the café,' he grunts. A small, shabby hovel not too far from Elif's house where men sit around drinking *çay* and discussing politics all day long. She hates it when he goes there, and he knows it.

Elif's eyes dash between my face and his. She's choosing who to disappoint. Feeling sorry for her, I'm about to offer to leave when she speaks, '*Güle güle.*'

With that, he's gone. We hear the car start up in the driveway.

I often wonder whether Elif is happy with Deniz, whether she doesn't regret getting married at nineteen. But I don't say anything to her. What would be the point? Other than making her sad.

'Sorry about that,' Elif says.

I just smile, pretending I haven't noticed a thing.

'Where were we?' she asks. 'Oh yes, the dress *Anne* bought you . . .'

'Did she . . .' I start. 'Did she also get a headscarf?'

Elif nods slowly and I turn my head away from her. 'If you don't want to wear it, you just have to tell her. It's not like she's going to force you.'

Chewing my bottom lip, I look at her. 'That's just the thing, though. I don't know what I want.'

'You don't have to make your decision now. You've got plenty of time.'

'You wore one once, remember? For a short while. I think I'd just started primary school and I thought you were so grown up. What made you take it off again?'

'I tried it for about three months, yes. I must've been about fifteen, I suppose. All my friends were wearing headscarves and I tried it out, more to fit in than anything else. It wasn't really a conscious decision or anything.'

'So why did you take it off?'

'I didn't feel comfortable with it. It wasn't me. I wanted to be more . . . more modern, I think. I honestly thought not wearing a headscarf was modern.'

'You're saying it isn't?'

'I don't know. Look at me. I'm twenty-five. I'm a housewife with two kids. I didn't study after school. If I should ever need to get a job, I have no idea what I'd do. Clean other people's houses? Sit behind a cash register? Not much more than that, I'm afraid. Does that strike you as a modern woman?'

She looks old and tired as she speaks. I've never seen her look this way before. Elif's always so busy, so positive, so friendly. 'But aren't you . . . aren't you happy?' I ask.

'That's not what I'm saying. I love Deniz, despite his faults, and I can't picture my life without the little ones, but I'm not sure this is who I imagined I'd be when I was your age. It's . . . it's the things you *do* that make you modern, Zey, not the things you wear.'

I'm shocked to see a tear run down her cheek. Impatiently, she wipes it away. I get up and go to sit down next to her. I want to take her hand but I know she's not really into soppy shows of affection. She doesn't like pity. So I just sit quietly for the longest time. At last she looks at me and smiles. She's composed herself and shoved her moment of sadness somewhere deep down inside. I wonder how long she'll leave it there.

I feel it's all right to ask my question now: 'So you don't think I should wear a headscarf?'

'You have to do what feels right for you. Follow your heart and all that. It's between you and Allah. It's got nothing to do with the rest of us.'

'But I don't know, Elif. I don't know what to decide, that's the problem.'

'Yes, but you're smart. You'll figure it out, and when you do, you'll be strong enough to stick to your decision. I'm sure about that.'

There's nothing more I can say. I know she thinks she's helped me, but instead I'm just more confused.

She pats me on the thigh. 'Come on, it's time for you to get back home.'

I groan. 'Do I have to?'

'Hold on. I've got something for you before you leave.'

Elif disappears down the passage to her bedroom. A minute later she's back and pushes something into my hand. It's her old mobile.

'So you can let us know where you are,' she says. 'You ought to know better than to pull a stunt like this afternoon, not telling *Anne* where you were. It doesn't work like that, Zey, and you know it.'

When I get home, I stand dead still in the empty lounge, thinking about Elif's advice, about her tears. I can hear my parents talking in subdued tones in the kitchen. Their voices go quiet because they've heard my footsteps. I'm concentrating so hard on what they're doing, I've stopped breathing. They're waiting. Probably expecting me to walk into the kitchen, in tears, begging forgiveness.

No, I can't do this. It's too hard. All their expectations, their anticipation, the weight of it is simply too much. No, I'm not going to give them what they want. What have I done that's so bad anyway? What have I done to deserve this? I went to my best friend's birthday party instead of going shopping for a stupid dress! Wow! Is that so bad? The crime of the century? The longer I stand here listening to their silence, the angrier I become.

I cough loudly, hoping they'll hear because this is the closest I'll actually come to being rude, and stomp noisily through the lounge and up to my bedroom. I close my door loudly too. Loud is good right now. I don't actually slam it, because young girls and slamming doors don't go together in our house. Not unless I want my phone taken away for a month, like they did the last time I tried it.

My shattered mobile is still lying on the floor. As I go to pick up the pieces, my eyes fall on a parcel on my bed. A small, square thing about the size of a book, wrapped in brown paper and neatly sealed with sticky tape. The baby hairs on the back of my neck, under my ponytail, bristle. Why are they giving me presents? I stare at it for a second or two before deciding to ignore it.

Going through the pieces, I search for my SIM card and shove it into Elif's old phone. It might as well have come from last century for all it's worth – it doesn't even have Wi-Fi. I plug it into the charger and then into the socket in the wall.

I switch it on.

The parcel on the bed is looking at me. I ignore it.

The phone asks me for the password. I punch in 1111 because I know Elif wouldn't have bothered changing her password once she'd brought it home from the shop. I'm right – the password is accepted.

Quickly I look over at the bed. And away again.

The phone wakes up. Many missed calls. One from an unfamiliar number. Maybe it was Alex? My finger hovers over the 'call back' button, then over 'delete'. What would I say to him anyway? *Hey, Alex, I just wanted to make sure this was your number?* He'll think I'm an idiot. No, I'll deal with that later.

There are some missed calls from Elif. Some from Kelly from yesterday. From before the episode in the bicycle shed at school. It feels so long ago I can hardly believe our fight only happened this morning. My throat tightens when I realize Kelly hasn't called me since. Hasn't texted me. Hasn't forgiven me. Quickly I push this thought to the back of my mind too.

I look at the bed instead.

The parcel is looking straight back at me.

I would swear out loud at this point – *if* I was that kind of girl. But I'm the kind of girl I am, and that's the problem. I know that swearing out loud or even softly to myself will always be heard by at least one other Being. So I don't. I just sit here on my knees in front of this stupid phone, not swearing, and staring at the parcel on the bed. I'm *wishing*, though, wishing very hard I was the kind of girl who *could* swear when everything got too much.

Finally, out of frustration, not knowing what else to do, I get up, go over to my bed and pick up the parcel. I place it gingerly on my lap. It's not a book. It's soft, thin.

A part of me knows exactly what's inside.

Carefully I take off the brown paper and it is just as I expected. A headscarf.

Except it's beautiful.

It's a very light blue colour, almost white, made of a sheer material, so delicate it looks like if you breathe on it, a hole will appear. The edges are embroidered with a fine, cobweb-like stitch and every couple of centimetres there is the tiniest of pearls. It looks ancient, though the little ticket with cleaning instructions sewn in one corner tells me it's not. It looks fragile. It is the loveliest thing I've ever held in my hands.

Anne has really outdone herself.

Without thinking, I'm up. I'm stumbling out of my room, the headscarf still clutched in my hands, down the stairs and into the kitchen. *Baba* and *Anne* are at the table, staring at me with their mouths open.

'It's beautiful, *Anne*,' I say in a breathy voice.

Before I remember I'm cross with them.

Before I remember they're cross with me.

My mum's face softens and a smile threatens to soften her lips too. She's trying hard to keep it at bay. My father's lips are pressed together.

I can't.

I can't stand here and look at them and hold this beautiful thing in my hands and be angry with them. Have them ignore me. Have them feel betrayed by me.

I can't.

Rushing over to the table, I sit down next to my father and reach for his hand. Holding it both of mine, I bring it up to my lips. I kiss the back of his hand. 'I'm sorry, *Baba*. I'm sorry that I lied to you.'

Quickly I lift my eyes to meet my mum's and then I drop them again. 'I'm sorry, *Anne*.'

I sit and wait. My eyes are fixed on the plastic table-cloth printed with baskets of blue flowers. At last, at very long last, I feel a movement in my father's body and the next thing I know his huge hand touches the back of my head. It feels exactly like his hand has always felt on the back of my head. It feels exactly right.

'You know being sorry doesn't have to be a bad thing, Zeyneb?'

'I know, *Baba*, I know.'

'As long as you learn something from it.'

His hand is still on the back of my bent head. I nod. I've heard this so many times before.

'But it's time to come clean, *kizim*, and tell us what really happened yesterday.'

Tears running down my cheeks, my nose running, yet smiling through it, I lift my head and tell my parents everything. *Anne* passes me a paper towel. I blow my nose and carry on talking. I tell them about the party and my sense of obligation to my best friend, about how I hate shopping and frilly, flashy dresses and gushing female relatives. I tell them everything.

Almost everything.

I don't tell them about Alex.

6

'What are you doing here?' Kelly freezes when she sees me.

I'm waiting for her by the bicycle rack in the car park of the building. Behind it is a small patch of garden where the residents are supposed to sit when they want fresh air, but no one seems to be taking care of it. Kelly has come down to get her bike for school and she's not expecting to find me here.

'I've got a new phone,' I say hopefully, holding it out for her to see. 'Well, not new, obviously. It's Elif's old phone. I mean, you can text me again . . . if you need to.'

'I don't need to text you, Zeyneb,' Kelly says, walking right past me.

It's cold for an April morning. There's a thin layer of frost covering the cars outside and our breath turns to water vapour as we stand here shivering. I've been up since dead early because I wanted to make sure I caught Kelly before she left for school.

'I . . . I . . . I . . .' But I can't find my words.

She goes to her bike, bends down and starts fiddling with the lock.

I take a deep breath. 'I'm sorry, Kel. I really am. I had no right to say those things to you.'

I wait. For a long time.

Crouched down, she doesn't look at me when she finally speaks. 'So why did you? Why'd you say I had no real family? Is that what you think about me?'

'Because . . . because I . . . because I'm an idiot. And I was angry with my parents so I took it out on you. I'm sorry.'

'Oh no.' She looks up and gives a disbelieving laugh. 'I'm not letting you get away with that one. One little "sorry" is supposed to wipe out everything you said?'

Pulling back my shoulders, I lift my head. I've never really explained things to Kelly before, about my family – well, not in depth anyway. I've never told her about respect and shame and expectations. Not because she doesn't know about these things, or doesn't believe in them, but because we look at it differently from other people. I'm going to be brave.

'Because I lied to my parents about going to your party and they found out and made a really big deal out of it. Because sometimes it's just so complicated being in my family that I can't find the words to tell you about it. Because I've got parents, a sister, aunts, cousins – you name it – who I have to take into account practically every time I move.'

'Just because you've got a big family, Zeyneb, doesn't

mean it's more complicated than mine. Or more real,' she says, standing up.

'No, no, it doesn't. I was wrong to say that. But with you, when you get older you're allowed to do more things, allowed more freedom. With us, it's exactly the opposite. The older we get the less we're allowed to do, the more we have to take everyone else into account. It just feels so unfair. I look at you with your mum and she's so cool and sometimes I get jealous at how easy your life is.'

Tears spill out of my friend's eyes. I'm horrified. Tough-Girl-Kelly never cries. I mean *never*. All the other girls in our class have cried at some point or another, about bad marks on a test or getting dumped by a boy, but never Kelly.

'*My* life is easy? *My* life? You must be joking. I look at you and think how nice it must be to go home after school and have your mum waiting for you with a plate of food she's spent hours cooking. I go home and heat up a tin of soup. Sometimes I can't fall asleep at night because I hear my mum crying in the room next door and I wish my father was here. Does that sound easy to you? Does that sound like something to be jealous of?'

I take a step towards her and she takes a step back.

'But you . . . you never . . . you never say anything . . .'

'Just like you. What do you ever tell me about *your* family?'

'I will. I won't keep things from you. I mean it. But then you also have to tell me when things get hard for you.'

47

She nods through her tears.

By now I'm crying too. 'I'm sorry, Kel. I shouldn't have said those things but I can't go back to yesterday and take them back.'

Sniffing loudly, she wipes her nose with the back of her hand. 'Can you stop feeling sorry for yourself long enough to realize that other people have problems too? Can you actually stop and think about how lucky you are?'

I'm nodding like my head's going to fall off, the snot and tears running down my face. I'll do anything she asks me right now so long as she'll forgive me.

Kelly does this funny little movement with her hands which I take to mean we're friends again. I step towards her and this time she lets me throw my arms around her. She hugs me back. Our last sniffles dry up and we compose ourselves.

'You ready for that French test today?' she asks when we finally get on our bikes.

'Oh, no . . .'

7

I look up at the clock on the wall in front of the class. Just twenty minutes to go before the bell. Mr Rubens has a meeting and he's left us alone for the last period. We've got a stack of Maths exercises to finish by tomorrow. I'm sitting in the third row from the front, behind Kelly. Alex is behind me, but I know he's watching me. Not all the time, like a stalker or anything, but every now and then. How do I know this? I just do. Obviously I don't turn round to look at him, because that would be giving myself away, but there's this spot on my back that goes all warm every couple of minutes and I *know* it's because he's looking at me.

Christine's playing a song on her mobile and she and Julie are practising the steps to some dance next to Mr Rubens' desk.

'Kelly, you want to join us?' Christine calls.

'Not now,' Kelly says, gesturing to the book I gave her for her birthday, which is open in front of her.

'Zeyneb?'

I shake my head. As if I'm the kind of girl who'll get up and start dancing in front of the class. Especially with Alex behind me! I look back down at my Maths.

'Come on,' Christine says. 'You can finish that at home.'

'No, seriously,' I say. 'I can't dance.'

They turn their attention to the next girl.

Mustafa and David are huddled together a few desks in front of me. They think they're whispering, but I hear them perfectly clearly.

'And Celeste?' David asks.

I see their eyes move shiftily over to where Celeste is sitting.

'Five or six,' Mustafa says.

'Six. Six. Definitely a six.' David nods in agreement and jots something down in the book in front of him.

'Nicole?'

Giving girls scores? Freaks. And anyway, Celeste is definitely worth more than a six – she's really pretty. Then I catch myself – what am I doing? I'm worse than they are.

I try to focus on my homework again.

'Zeyneb?' I hear David's voice.

Raising my head, I glare at the two of them. 'Just you dare,' I call across.

They stare at me for a second before huddling even closer together and whispering something. They laugh loudly.

I'm really angry with them. I think about what Kelly

would do, and I push back my chair and walk over to the two of them. Before they realize I'm there, I'm bending down behind them, my mouth close to their ears. 'Get a life,' I say loudly.

They're startled and jerk upright at the same time. I hear a dull thud as their foreheads knock together.

'Ow!' While they're rubbing their foreheads I stretch over and grab the book. There, one below the other, are the names of all the girls in our class: Julie, Christine, Kelly, Celeste, Nicole, Zeyneb . . . Next to my name I see a 7.5.

It makes me feel confused but I push that out of the way. What exactly do they think we are? A bunch of cattle at the market? Tearing out the page, I crumple it up and toss the book back down in front of them.

'Hey, that's my Maths book,' David complains.

'Well, use it for Maths, then,' I reply before going back to my desk.

Behind me I hear someone chuckling. It's Alex. 'What were they doing?' he asks me.

I turn round to him. 'Giving the girls marks out of ten.'

'Idiots,' he says.

I nod, secretly pleased.

'How much did they give you?'

I shrug – not wanting to say. But I guess he'll find out. 'Seven-and-a-half.'

'Only seven-and-a-half! What? Are they blind or something?'

Quickly I turn back to my book so he doesn't see me

blushing. Alex thinks I'm more than a seven-and-a-half! I can't believe it. I'm sitting here, grinning, my hand in front of my mouth so no one can see.

At last I hear his voice again. 'You want to help me with this exercise?'

Of course I want to help him, even though there's not a cell in my body that believes he can't do it. He's the only one in class who gets higher marks than me for Maths. But then another part of me doesn't want to help him at all. I know it's just a ruse to get me to sit down next to him and he's the one boy in the world I should *not* be sitting next to!

Turning round to look at him, I try to sound non-chalant: 'Which one?'

'Number eight. Am I supposed to change this negative into a positive before I multiply it, or should I just leave it?'

One or two kids have stopped what they're doing and they're listening to our exchange. I don't want their eyes on us. Their always-questioning, always-looking-for-more-than-there-is eyes. *Stop looking!* I want to yell, but of course I don't.

'Don't know, Alex. I haven't got to that question yet,' I lie.

I drop my eyes back to the page in front of me and try to disappear from the spotlight. At the same time, I can't bear the thought of our conversation ending. My stomach churns just from wanting to hear him say something else to me. Hear him call me again, *Hey, Zeyneb.*

The numbers on my page are one big blur.

A chair scrapes and then all of a sudden I smell him right there behind me. The scent of his faded deodorant mixed with mint – he's chewing gum. I can feel the heat of his body right through my clothes. His hand appears over my shoulder as he drops his exercise book on the desk in front of me. He's pulling up a chair. He sits down and, leaning towards me, supposedly to concentrate on the book, his thigh touches mine beneath the desk.

I jump a mile high and move as far away from him as possible until I'm squashed up against the table leg. But his face is still far too close and his left arm is casually slung over the back of my chair.

'This one here,' he says, pointing to the page.

The answer's already been filled in: 375. 21. It's the same as mine. Can he hear my heart beating like this?

I pick up my pen, bend my head and pretend to focus on the sum. I'm petrified.

'I tried to phone you, but you didn't pick up,' he says, his voice soft and close to my ear. I feel his breath on my neck. *Don't scream, Zeyneb. Don't scream!* I don't look at him.

So the unknown number *was* his. 'I was . . . um . . . having trouble with my phone.'

He's looking at me sideways now, his fringe flopping over one eye. 'I wanted to ask if you . . . if you maybe wanted to go to the funfair with me?'

I bite down hard on my bottom lip, so hard I taste blood. It's either that or I start crying right here in front of him. I can't believe I have to say these words: 'I can't, Alex.'

'Why not?'

'Because I'm not allowed to . . .'

'Not allowed to go to the funfair?'

'Not allowed to go with a boy,' I whisper.

His hand moves along the back of my chair and his fingers touch my back. I sit up dead straight. It feels like his fingers have burned a hole right through my T-shirt and my skin is on fire. Skin is not supposed to feel like this, I tell myself sternly.

'You're *never* allowed to go anywhere with a boy?' He sounds curious now.

'Well, sometimes. I mean, in a group or something. Like if I was going out with the whole class to the cinema. They wouldn't really mind about that.'

'Can't you just say you're going with the whole class?'

'I can't lie to my parents, Alex. I really can't.'

'Then we'll go in a group. You ask Kelly, Julie and Celeste. I'll ask some of the boys. And then we'll be OK, won't we?'

'I don't know. It still feels kind of dishonest.'

'If you come, I'll prove to you we can go out as friends. Promise.'

I can't help but laugh at him. 'I'm not sure if I'll be allowed to go.'

'Come on, say yes,' he says.

'Why do you need an answer right now?'

'Y – E – S. Come on, say it.' He's laughing. Gently. And

even though I'm not looking at him, I know those white teeth and that dimple are doing their thing and the Awe and Wonder is melting me, turning my insides into mush.

So I look at him. Quickly. For less than a second, because that's all I've got the courage for. He's looking back at me. I want his fingers to touch my back again. I want his thigh to brush against mine. I want him to look away, to go away. I want him to look at me like this for ever.

'I'll see,' I say at last.

'Will you let me know?'

I nod.

'When?'

'Just go away!'

'When?' he insists.

'I'll text you, OK?'

'When?'

'Idiot.' I laugh, and so does he.

The bell rings then, and I've never been so relieved to hear it in my entire life.

8

Yesterday was a really good day. Well, good and bad at the same time. First Alex asked me to the funfair and that was good, but at the same time it was bad. Because it means I'm thinking about lying to my parents again. Some of the time I'm convinced I'm going to do the right thing and tell Alex I can't go, and then I'm really proud of myself. But then I remember his smile, or playing football with him in the park, or the fact that he thinks I'm worth more than a seven-and-a-half, and all my good resolutions go flying out the window again.

Last night, when I got home from school, my parents told me my grandmother, *Baba*'s mum, had decided to fly in from Turkey for my cousin's wedding. *Baba* left for the airport early this morning to fetch her. I begged him to take me with, but he wouldn't let me skip school.

But she's here now and I'm sitting on the floor in her bedroom, my shoulders against her knees, my hair let loose from my ponytail. She's on her bed and she's plaiting my hair. This is what we do when *Babaanne* comes to visit. Every time.

After all the fussing and gushing are over – the exchange of gifts behind us, the tea and cake guzzled – *Babaanne* asks me to go to her room to help her unpack. Then we sit like this. She does my hair as she used to do her sisters' hair when they were young (she never had a daughter of her own), and we catch up.

'I need to ask you something,' I start in Turkish, the only language she speaks. She's the one person in my family, besides Elif, who I can ask questions without her going into meltdown. It's like the young and the old can listen, but the ones in the middle absolutely can't. I wonder if I'll become like that when I reach the middle? Was *Babaanne* ever like that?

'What is it, *kizim*?' she says.

My hair, which hangs halfway down my back, is being tugged and pulled in all directions as the plait progresses. It hurts, but not unbearably, so I say nothing. Her knees are poking into my back and I'm not exactly what you'd call comfortable, but I wouldn't want to be anywhere else in the world right now. The whole room smells like earth. Dry earth. Dust. It's the smell *Babaanne* carries around with her everywhere – the smell of her garden.

She lives in a little house halfway up a hill in a dry, dusty village. It's where *Baba* lived when he was a boy. There's this long, winding pot-holed road that leads up to it and as you go round the final bend and the village comes into view, you immediately spot her house. All the other houses are dirty white, grey or brown and kind of blend in with the rocky background. Not hers. It sticks out, literally, for miles. There are flowers everywhere in her garden. The dark pink flowers of the bougainvillea cover half of the house. There are yellow daisies and red roses and hardy pink geraniums. She has flowers that people in Turkey don't even *think* about planting. We're constantly sending her little packets of seeds in the post and she coaxes them into splendour with loads of attention and water. A few years ago my father had to pay for a borehole to be drilled in her back yard so she'd have enough water for her plants. In between all the flowers she grows courgettes, aubergines, red peppers, cucumbers, pumpkins, tomatoes, onions and carrots – practically a whole vegetable shop.

She also has chickens and geese and a couple of goats she keeps for milk. Once one of the goats managed to get out of its pen and started munching away at her flowers. That weekend she had a feast and invited all her neighbours and they ate spit-roasted goat. Some of the men from the village fixed the fence and *Babaanne* made sure it was safer than a maximum-security prison before she bought a new goat. Her flowers were not going to fall victim to another one.

My grandmother came to live with us a few years ago but she only lasted a couple of months. Couldn't get used to it here. The cars and the shops and the television. It's not like they don't have those things in Turkey. Of course they do, but they just aren't a part of *Babaanne*'s everyday existence. It's like what they say about not replanting old trees. Well, *Babaanne* is a very old, very big tree and she simply couldn't be replanted here.

If there's one thing *Babaanne* loves even more than her garden, it's dancing. Put on any kind of music and she'll start moving – tapping her toes, swaying her hips ever so slightly, clicking her fingers, moving her head . . . My father says when she was young she was the best dancer from many, many villages. People would go quiet when she started dancing.

Now she's got this bad hip and she gets around with a walking stick, but it's still impossible to keep her still. Put on a good Turkish song and she's lost to it. She gets up and starts dancing right there, leaning on her walking stick, sometimes wincing from the pain, but dancing all the same. I swear, you've never seen anything like it.

'Tell me what's bothering you,' *Babaanne* says now, tugging at a strand of hair. 'I see your shoulders are tense, and so are the muscles in your neck.'

Two strong fingers take hold of the back of my neck and start kneading. I cringe because in a way it hurts, but at the same time it feels good.

'Did you ever wear a headscarf, *Babaanne*?'

My grandmother has long black hair, streaked with grey. She ties it up in a tight bun on the top of her head. Like many other Turkish women, she chooses not to wear a headscarf. Nowadays in Turkey it's seen as old-fashioned, as conservative, even backwards by some people. Many more women wear headscarves here than they do back in Turkey. Elif says it's because they can't let go of the old country, because they're clinging on to an ideal that doesn't exist any more. *Anne* says it's holding on to tradition in a society with different values.

'I did, a long time ago, when I was a young girl, a little older than you,' *Babaanne* says. 'All the women used to wear headscarves back then.'

'What did it feel like?'

'What did it *feel* like?' she repeats. 'Mmm, let me think. It felt like a kind of protection. Not from the sun or anything, though there was that too, but from . . . How can I say it? From the bad things in this world. It was like a very loud and clear message to everyone: *this is a good girl. She comes from a good family. Her religion is important to her. Do not come close with any evil.* Yes, that's more or less what it felt like.'

'But that's a good feeling, isn't it?' I ask, confused. It sounds as if wearing a headscarf has nothing but advantages, so why is her head uncovered?

'It is a good feeling, Zeyneb.'

'Then why did you stop if it made you feel safe?'

'Feeling safe *is* a good thing, child, but . . .' She pauses.

'But what?'

'Think of a herd of gazelle,' she says.

'A herd of gazelle?'

'Yes, remember when you came to visit last year we saw some of them?'

I nod.

'Well, in any herd like that, half of the animals are in a state of constant alertness. They're aware of every sound,

60

every sprig of grass that snaps, always ready to bolt. These gazelles are very important in the herd. They keep it safe. But then you have the other kind. The ones that venture out a little bit further than is safe, the ones that risk being eaten by a bear or a wolf in exchange for greener, sweeter grass. And, mind you, these are the ones that get eaten most often. The bolters, the careful ones, hardly ever end up as someone's supper. But the point is that, for the herd to survive, it needs both types of gazelle. The careful ones that keep the herd safe, and the risk-takers that find new fields of grass.'

She keeps quiet and lets me think. 'So, you're one of the gazelles that find green grass?' I say eventually.

'Yes, I think that's the kind I am.'

'And that's why you stopped wearing a headscarf?'

'Well, no, not exactly.' She laughs. 'I had no idea what kind of gazelle I was in those days. I was just a baby gazelle really, like you are now – a follower – and I simply did what all the others did.'

'What made you take it off?'

'I was out working in the fields with my sisters one day, we were harvesting the chickpea crop. We'd taken our goat with us so we could have fresh milk at lunchtime. She was tethered to a tree but somehow she managed to get loose and, the next thing I know, she's standing next to me and she tries to take a bite out of my headscarf. It was green, so maybe she thought it was grass, I don't know. Anyway, she pulls the whole thing off my head and eats it. There was nothing I could do. It was too far for me to go back home for a new one, so I found a piece of string, tied up my long hair, and carried on picking chickpeas – after my sisters had finished laughing at me, of course.

'And you know what, it turned out it was much easier working without a cumbersome headscarf round my face and shoulders all day, much cooler. I never put one on again after that day.'

'What did your parents say?'

'They weren't happy, of course. They were worried about what the family and the neighbours would say. They were worried that no decent boy would want to marry me. They made my life very difficult for a while, but I stuck to my decision. I was exactly the same girl without my headscarf on. I still respected my parents, I didn't run around with boys, so, after a while, everyone just got used to it and the worst they called me in the end was stubborn. And they were right, I was stubborn. But stubborn's not always a bad thing.'

'What happened? Did any decent boy want to marry you?'

'*Kizim*, do you think I sat around waiting for the sweet green grass to find me? No, *I* found a decent boy *I* wanted to marry. It took a while, though. It was years later that I met your grandfather. All my sisters were already married and my parents were convinced they were going to be stuck with me for ever.'

'And me, *Babaanne*, what kind of gazelle do you think I am?'

'Only you know the answer to that question. No one else.'

'But I don't, that's the problem.'

'It's a problem?'

'Yes, I don't know *who* I am.'

'No, you've got it the wrong way round. Getting to know who you are is one of the pleasures in this life, not a problem.'

I smile because I know she wants me to smile, even though she can't see my face. I smile because she said the word *pleasure* and we're all supposed to smile when we hear that word, but for once I don't agree with *Babaanne* as wholeheartedly as I usually do. Maybe it was all a pleasure for her when she was my age, but it definitely isn't for me.

9

It's Friday afternoon. My favourite time of the week. School's finished. No homework. My mum, *Babaanne* and I have done our ritual wash and said our prayers. *Anne* is busy cooking a big meal for when *Baba* gets back from the mosque. Elif and the kids are also coming round for dinner, but I won't be eating with them tonight.

I'm allowed to go to the cinema with Kelly! Yay!

I had to beg my parents for practically an hour before they said yes. We're going to see that film everyone's raving about.

I'm in my bedroom, getting ready. Jeans and a clean T-shirt. Standing in front of the mirror, I make sure my hair is OK. My eyes fall on my headscarf lying folded up on the dressing table. I pick it up and wrap it around my head. Just to see what it looks like. Feel what it feels like. I frown at the girl staring back at me, then I go into *Anne*'s bedroom and take another headscarf from her cupboard, a dark-blue one. Back in front of the mirror, I put the dark one on first and then the one my mum bought me.

A double headscarf.

I've noticed lots of girls wearing their headscarves like this lately, this two-toned effect swirled together to create a sophisticated look. This is what I'm aiming for, but instead my creation looks like two floor rags balanced on my head. I wish there was someone who could show me how to do this. I'd go to *Babaanne*'s room next door and ask her, but I doubt she's very up-to-date on the latest headscarf fashion. And my mum – well, let's just say the one person I do *not* want to look like is her. Her headscarves are usually floral prints. Yuk! She won't know a thing about arranging a double headscarf.

I hear the doorbell downstairs, and a few seconds later my mum's voice at the door.

'Good evening, Mrs Ozturk,' Kelly says, sounding all formal and stiff.

'It's good to see you. Zeyneb is upstairs in her room.'

I hear Kelly's footsteps on the stairs, quiet and respectful, not like at school where she takes them two at a time, always in a rush. I thought it was physically impossible for Kelly to climb stairs like a normal person.

My hands fly up to the ill-constructed headscarves to take them off, but Kelly barges into my room before I do so. 'Come on, dork. The bus is coming in fifteen . . .'

She stops and stares at me.

Turning away from the mirror, I face her. I'm biting my bottom lip.

'You're going to wear *that*?' she says in disbelief.

'What?' I ask tentatively, glancing at the floor before

looking up to meet her eyes.

'The headscarf. Since when have you . . .'

'You think I shouldn't wear one?'

Kelly looks me up and down like she's seeing me for the first time. Her forehead is creased, her eyes big. 'I don't know. I didn't realize you were into . . . all of this.'

'I'm just trying it on. Trying to decide, you know . . .'

'Decide what?'

'If I'm going to be one of those girls who wears a headscarf.'

I wait for a response. Shock. Laughter. Nothing. She just stares at me.

'Well, are you?' she finally says.

I shrug. 'I don't know yet. What do you think?'

'I don't know. I'm probably the last person you should be asking for advice.'

'But you're not. You're my friend and what you think is important to me.'

'I don't *know*, Zey. I don't know what I think. I've never thought of you like this before.'

'You think it's dumb?'

'I don't suppose it's dumb exactly, it's just . . .'

'Just what?'

'I guess I could get used to it if that's what you really want to do, but . . . well, it might make a difference to other people.'

'What difference?'

She walks into my room and sits down on my bed. 'How people will see you and all.'

'How will they see me?'

Kelly shrugs. She's not looking at me. 'Without a headscarf people think you're a modern girl. That's what they're always saying, at least. But with one they'll think you're, you know, one of those girls who can't think for themselves, someone who lets men tell her what to do. Some people might think it's radical.'

'But that's not true,' I wail. 'I'm not trying to be radical.'

'*I* know it's not true. *You* know it's not true. But other people will walk around thinking *their* opinions are true. That's just the way it is.'

I pull the headscarves off my head, scrunch them up and stuff them under my pillow. Kelly's eyes follow my movements. For once I'm not sure what she's thinking.

'You think I shouldn't do it, then?' I ask, biting my lip again.

'What I think is that we're going to miss the bus if you don't get a move on.'

'Do you think I should wear a headscarf?' I insist.

'I think you could try it just to see what it feels like. Then you can decide for yourself.'

I grin at her. She grins back, but it's an awkward grin and I don't know how to make it not awkward.

Turning away from her, I glance in the mirror to check my hair. I nod and the two of us go downstairs. My mum's waiting at the front door.

'Bye, *Anne*,' I say.

'Be careful and don't be late. Your father will be there to pick you up at eight. Wait at the entrance where there's enough light,' she says. 'Do you need any money?'

Shaking my head, I kiss her cheek and then we're out the door.

'You're mad,' Kelly says.

'What do you mean?'

'You should always say yes if someone offers you money.' She laughs. 'Dork!'

Clutching my box of popcorn and my Coke, I'm trying to find the right screen. 'It was number nine, wasn't it?' I ask Kelly.

She's not next to me any more. About five paces behind, she's come to a standstill. 'Look who's here,' she says in a slow, meaningful voice.

I scan the crowd but I can already guess who it is from the tone of her voice. My heart plummets into my shoes and my stomach gets that heavy, grinding feeling. I don't want him to be here. I don't want to have to speak to him and smile at him and feel myself go all fluttery inside. I don't want to do this to my parents after what happened last Sunday.

Four boys are huddled together by the Charlie Chaplin painting on the wall. David, Jamal and Matt from our class, and of course *him*. Right in the middle, sticking out as if he's been lit up with a thousand light bulbs – smile, eyes, dimple and all.

His eyes meet mine before I can look away. My stomach jumps into my throat. The other guys are nudging him, laughing, but his face stays serious and he simply stares at me across the carpeted cinema foyer. He's not paying any attention to his idiot friends – except when they start moving towards us, as a group, as if they've practised it. It's almost as if they're in some old-fashioned cowboy film or something – they walk the same walk, legs apart slightly more than is necessary, an exaggerated spring in their step. The walk all boys use when they're trying to look cool. The walk girls laugh about behind their backs.

Except Alex, of course. He has no walk. He's positively gliding towards me. Gliding! I swear, I've never seen anything like it.

Wrenching my eyes away from him, I nudge Kelly urgently. 'Come on, let's go inside so we can get a good seat.' I'm picturing two lone seats between two sets of strangers, with no place for other people to join us unless they sit on our laps.

'Watch out!' Kelly calls. I've knocked her arm and she's spilled her drink all over herself.

'I'm sorry!'

'Here, hold this,' she says, irritated, and thrusts her drink into my hands. 'I'm going to the bathroom to wash this off.'

'Kelly, no . . .' I call after her, but she's already gone.

I hardly dare turn my attention back to the boys, but at the same time I know I can't afford not to. They've stopped. The whole group has come to a standstill. No cool walk. No gliding. All eight eyes fixed on me. I'm standing in the middle of the foyer, clutching two huge drinks and a box of popcorn, looking like one of *Babaanne*'s gazelles staring down the barrel of a gun. Alex is saying something to them. Jamal nods. Matt and David laugh, and then Alex starts gliding again. Towards me. On his own.

I want to run. Want to drop everything right here on the floor and charge into another cinema showing some boring drama that only old people watch, just so no one can follow me. But I don't. I stand here. Clutching. Watching. While Alex glides.

He stops in front of me. He's smiling, and the Awe and Wonder are threatening to break out again. I know I won't be able to say anything if they do.

'Get a grip, Zeyneb,' I tell myself.

'What?' says Alex.

OMG! Did I say that out loud? I feel myself blush like I've never blushed before.

His forehead is knotted and his head is tilted slightly to one side.

'Kelly's gone to the ladies'. She has to wash her hands so they won't be sticky,' I say.

What am I talking about?

He nods but looks confused now. 'Which film are you going to see?'

I tell him the name of the film. Too fast. Of course they're going to see the same film, I realize. Too late. Why didn't I say something else? Why didn't I lie? Or ask him which film he was going to see first? Why can't I think before I open my big mouth?

'Us too,' he says, and jerks his head in the direction of the others standing there staring at us. 'Celeste and Julie are here as well.'

He waits for me to say something. But what?

'Kelly's gone to the bathroom,' I repeat.

Who is this idiot who's taken over my mouth? What is wrong with me?

'You want to sit together?' he asks.

I shake my head, furiously. 'I can't, Alex. I told you the other day, I'm not allowed—'

'You said your parents wouldn't mind if you were in a group,' he interrupts. 'Well, we're in a group, aren't we?'

I'm thinking about Elif and *Babaanne* sitting at the dining-room table at home, about the headscarf lying scrunched up beneath my pillow. I'm thinking about keeping-alert gazelles and new-green-grass gazelles and wondering whether girl gazelles find boy gazelles as gorgeous as I find Alex. I'm thinking this over and over again, but of course, instead of doing the right thing, I nod.

I'm saying yes.

I'm sorry, Baba. I'm sorry, Anne.

Alex smiles and suddenly it's as if the fast-forward button has been pressed. Kelly appears at my side. Jamal, David and Matt do the Walk over to us. Celeste and Julie are there saying hi and the next thing I know, we're inside the cinema, searching for eight empty places. There's a lot of joking going on as we shuffle awkwardly into one of the rows past sets of knees. I've made sure Kelly's right in front of me, but when I whip my head round to check behind me, Alex is there, grinning. Oh, no . . . what have I done?

I poke Kelly's shoulder, and give a 'help me' stare. 'What shall I do?' I mouth.

'Sit down, that's what,' she whispers back.

'But—'

'But nothing. Just sit down, Zey. It'll be fine.'

But will it?

There's nothing I can do without making a huge fuss. So I sit down.

Alex is next to me. Exactly where he shouldn't be. Exactly where *Baba* and *Anne* would expect another girl to be sitting. Or a stranger. Preferably a woman.

I draw in my elbows and shove my hands between my knees, resolving to let him have the armrest all to himself.

The music starts up, pouring ominously out of the speakers in the grey, carpeted walls, the lights go down and an image of an insanely happy man sipping a bottle of Coke appears on the screen. I'm chewing a piece of popcorn but it tastes like pure cement. My mouth is dry and I can't swallow. I clear my throat. I do it again but still the popcorn won't go down.

'Are you all right?' Alex whispers into my ear.

I jump. He's so close I feel his breath on my cheek. *Are you really doing this, Zeyneb? Sitting here in the dark letting this boy whisper into your ear?* The baby hairs on the back of my neck stand on end and a shiver runs over my shoulders. I gasp but that only causes me to start coughing, sending bits of popcorn flying out of my mouth.

'What's wrong?'

'I'm . . . I'm . . . I'm not feeling well.'

I can't do this – I *know* it's wrong. I can't sit here for the whole film and pretend everything's OK. It's not.

Without knowing what I'm doing, I jump up and start pushing my way out blindly, bashing into knees as I go, trying to get to the aisle, to get out of here. To get away from him. I think someone's following me, whispering something. *Please let it not be him!* I reach the last knees and push past them, stumbling on to the dark, carpeted steps. I feel two hands on my elbow, helping me up.

It's Kelly. The relief almost makes me want to cry.

She's got her hands on my shoulders, looking into my face, her eyes huge with worry. 'Zeyneb, what's wrong?'

'I can't do this,' I say. 'I'm going to catch the bus home.'

10

It's Monday, and Kelly and I are holed up in the school bathroom. I haven't seen her since running out of the cinema on Friday night. She went away for the weekend, visiting family with her mum, while I spent the whole weekend moping, trying to decide if I'd done the right thing or not. Would it have been better if I'd stayed calm and just waited till the end of the film? Would that have been so bad? Would I have been betraying my parents if I'd ignored Alex? Was it even possible for me to ignore Alex? All of these questions going round and round in my mind the whole time. They're making me crazy.

'What did Alex say?'

'Zey, do we have to go over this again? I've told you all of this over the phone.'

'Just once more, Kel, I promise.'

She sighs. 'OK, when I got back from walking you to the bus stop, he wanted to know what was wrong, if he'd said or done anything.'

'And?'

'And I told him you weren't feeling well, that you were coming down with something.'

'Did he believe you? I mean, when you looked into his face, did it look like he really, properly believed you?'

Kelly shrugs. 'It was dark, and honestly, no – he probably didn't believe me. You were acting so weird.'

Just like the first time she told me this, it stings. My eyes fill with tears. Alex thinks I'm weird. What am I going to do now? How do I make him believe I'm just like everyone else? Why didn't I just pretend to be sick this morning and stay at home? It would be easier than this.

I wish I was in *Baba*'s allotment right now, pulling up weeds or watering the seedlings. It helps me think. It's the one place where I feel calm, where I feel OK to be Zeyneb, no matter what.

We hear the clicking of heels outside and the bathroom door opens. It must be a teacher. Quickly I go to a basin and splash some water on my face.

'Come on, girls, I want you in the hall right away.'

It's Mrs Bickham, the careers tutor. It's the school's annual careers day and we're supposed to be in the hall, figuring out our future. But the only future I'm worried about is the rest of the day, and how to get to the end of it as quickly as possible.

Our school does this every year. They invite all these people from different organizations and colleges and the local university to come and talk to us. It's kind of silly, all these strangers huddled in our school hall, but then I suppose it makes us think about our futures and stuff like that. So maybe it's not completely dumb.

'Have you picked one yet?' Kelly asks. Because she's new she's not sure how it works.

I nod. 'And you?'

'I don't know. How're we supposed to know what we want to do years from now?'

'It's just to get an idea. It's not like you have to sign a contract or anything.'

Kelly shrugs. 'But I don't know . . .'

I can hear people making jokes about how boring it must be being an adult and going to the same stupid job every day of your life for the next hundred years or so. Probably, deep down, everyone's a bit scared because we know we'll *have* to choose soon. We can't stay kids for ever. And what happens if you choose the wrong thing and you only figure it out when you're ancient, like forty?

But no one actually says these things. Everyone's much too busy being cool and trying to come up with funny quips:

'Imagine . . . imagine being a funeral director but you're scared of dead people.'

'Or . . . or . . . or a window cleaner on one of those skyscrapers but you've got a fear of heights.'

Really lame. But sometimes lame's what we do so we can avoid talking about the big stuff.

The *stalls* – that's what the teachers call them – are just a bunch of tables pushed together. They're decorated with logos and leaflets and business cards and banners.

Some of the really fancy ones have flags or slideshows projected against the wall. Last year you could zip round really quickly, pick up a couple of leaflets and slip out again. But then some people got caught smoking behind the hall, so this year Mrs Bickham has changed the whole formula. We have to choose one career that interests us and kind of interview the person at that table. Afterwards we have to go home and write an essay about it, about the person, about why we chose that particular stall – that kind of thing – and present it in class the next week. We're going to get marked on it, too. But even though everyone's moaning about it, I actually don't mind.

This is because I know exactly which stand I'm going to: *Baba* always says, 'With a head like that on your shoulders, my girl, there's only one place for you – university.' He's dead proud when he says that, emphasizes the word *university* as if it's one of the best words in the world. I see his chest swell up and the way his eyes shine when he looks at me. You see, no one in our family has ever gone to university, not here nor in Turkey. I think the idea of it is very exciting. I've already got some questions I want to ask when I get to the stand. Then I can tell *Baba* all about it tonight when I get home.

'You want to come with me?' Kelly nudges me as we stand here, staring at the sea of strange adult faces.

'Do you know where you're going to go?'

'You know what . . .' Kelly hesitates. 'I thought maybe the army.'

My eyebrows shoot up in surprise. 'The army! Since when have you been interested in the army?'

I can see from the way she twists her ponytail that I'm making her feel unsure.

'But I'll come with you if you like,' I add, and her face breaks into a smile.

'Thanks, Zey.'

I follow Kelly to the stand where a couple of soldiers in uniform are standing around. I can't see Kelly dressed up like this in a couple of years, holding a gun, shooting people in wars. How horrible! But I don't say anything. It's not for me to choose, is it?

There's this lady soldier and Kelly's asking her all these questions. She's telling Kelly about all the different jobs you can do in the army, like being a medic or a chef or even a lawyer. I must say, I had no idea. I'm staring at her blonde hair as she talks to Kelly. I don't actually know if it's long or short because it's tucked up under her army beret. Her back's really straight and her chin is held high. It makes me think about *Anne* moaning at me, telling me not to slouch, and I stand up straight as I listen to them. They seem to be getting on really well.

' . . . the army will pay for your studies too,' she's telling Kelly.

'But do you really have to get up at five o'clock in the morning for the rest of your life?' Kelly asks.

The soldier laughs. 'Even earlier sometimes. That's very important in the army: discipline.'

'So, do you *never* get to sleep in?'

'Of course, on your days off you can sleep as late as you like.'

'You get days off?' Kelly asks, and again the woman laughs.

There aren't too many girls hanging out here so I imagine this lady soldier must be grateful to have Kelly to talk to. But, the problem is, the longer Kelly stands here, the less time I have to ask questions at *my* stand.

I nudge her. 'Kel, I'll catch up with you at break.'

Kelly nods, but she's not looking at me – all her attention is on the blonde soldier. I suppose it's not the *worst* idea in the world, Kelly going into the army. She seems really interested. It might even suit her.

I hurry across the hall to the university stand. Actually, they've got so much to say that they've been given two tables instead of just one like all the other organizations. Secretly I'm pleased. I think the university deserves two tables, but that's probably just because it's what I've chosen. I'm staring at the piles of brochures and leaflets and everything spread out in front of me. I have no idea where to start.

'You're thinking about going to university?' I hear a voice ask.

I look up at the woman behind the table, but . . . she's not what I expect to see. She's . . . well, she's olive-skinned, like me, and she's wearing a headscarf. A bright fuchsia-pink one, wrapped tightly around her face and neck in a way that's kind of modern-looking.

'Do you teach at the university?' I ask. I can hear the

79

shock in my voice and hope it doesn't sound rude.

'I lecture part-time, yes,' she says, 'but I also work for the Student Affairs department.'

'What's that?'

'Well, we do a whole lot of things. One of them, for instance, is to try to help students from underprivileged backgrounds to find a way to pay for their studies. Or to encourage pupils like you to take the step to go on to tertiary education.'

'Pupils like me? What do you mean?'

'Pupils from ethnic minorities,' she explains.

'I'm an *ethnic minority*?'

'Well, I assume so. Am I wrong?'

I've never thought of myself as an *ethnic minority*. I mean, I'm not stupid – of course I know there are fewer Muslim kids than the rest, but I never really made the leap that that made me an *ethnic minority*. I just figured I'm Zeyneb and I have to struggle along and do my best at school like everyone else. But maybe I'm not like everyone else at all. Or maybe I am, and the rest of the world is just making it more complicated than it actually is.

'What's your name?' asks the woman.

'Zeyneb.'

'I'm Zehra.' She stretches out her hand across the table. Gingerly I take it and give it an uncertain shake. I've never shaken hands with a grown-up before – it feels kind of cool.

'You're thinking about going to university when you've

finished school?' she tries again.

I nod vigorously.

'What would you like to study?'

'I don't know yet. Something really hard.'

She throws back her head and laughs. I shouldn't have said that, I realize, too late. I must sound really stupid. I blush.

'Which subjects are you good at?'

'Maths, science, biology. But I'm good at the other subjects too,' I blurt out before I realize that I'm sounding like a huge show-off.

But she doesn't seem fazed. 'Well, that's good. We definitely need more women in the sciences. What do you enjoy most?'

I hesitate, but then an image pops into my head of me helping *Baba* in the allotment every Saturday morning. Of lying under my hydrangea. Of watering the African violets on my windowsill. 'I like plants. Gardening.' I hesitate. 'That's not really a subject, I know. I'm sorry.'

'The study of plants – of course it's a subject. Botany is a highly respected field.'

'You mean I can spend three years just learning about plants?'

'Even longer, if you'd like to.' She smiles.

'Is that what you studied?'

Again she laughs. She must think I'm weird with all my stupid questions. 'No, I studied Social Sciences.'

'Social Sciences – what does that mean?'

'Psychology, sociology, criminology – things like that.'

'Studying the way we think, you mean?' I ask.

I'm expecting more laughter but instead she just smiles. This woman really isn't like anyone I expected to find behind the university table. 'Yes, I suppose that's one way to look at it,' she says.

'What . . . what do your parents think?'

'About . . . ?'

'About what you've studied? About doing this?'

'They're extremely proud, as any parent would be.'

I'm nodding. It's true. I can see why this woman's parents would be proud of her.

'And your parents? Do they know about your plans?' she asks, gently.

'My father *wants* me to go to university. He says Allah gave me the gift of intelligence so I have to make the most of it. But I haven't told him anything about Botany yet.'

'You know that means you won't necessarily get married straight after school, don't you?'

'But I don't want to get married straight after school,' I say.

'Does your father know that?'

I shrug, but I don't really know the answer. 'He loves gardening,' I say. 'He'll think Botany's a good idea, I'm sure.'

'Well, that's important, to have your family behind you with a big decision like this. Just make sure you discuss your plans carefully with them. You don't want any sudden surprises later on, do you?'

I shake my head. I suppose not. It's not really something I've thought about before. The only thing I'm sure about is that my parents will be proud of me the day I set off for university. Surely they won't expect me to do that *and* get married dead young like Elif? Or will they? Suddenly my stomach feels a little queasy.

I stand around talking to Zehra until the bell rings for break. At one point I realize Kelly's joined me. She's standing behind me, and this time she's the one not interested in our conversation. She's got her back to us and she's staring at the other kids in the hall. A little while later I hear Alex's voice. He's talking to some guy at the other end of the university table, something about meteorology. I'm so wrapped up in all the questions I'm rattling off to Zehra that, for once, I don't melt into a puddle of goo simply because he's standing a couple of paces away.

At last, I leave. Reluctantly. All Zehra's colleagues have started packing the leaflets into boxes, and I can see them looking at her like she should be helping them, so I go. Out to break, or what's left of it. With Kelly and the others. In my hands I clutch a bunch of leaflets Zehra gave me. And a business card.

'Botany,' I keep repeating to myself. 'A highly respected field.'

11

I'm sitting here in class, thinking about my conversation with Zehra at the university stand yesterday. About studying Botany, about becoming a botanist. Then I look at Mr Stein and wonder what on earth flashes across a person's brain to make them think, *Hey, I want to be a Geography teacher.*

He's going on about weather patterns and high pressure and low pressure. Looking around at everyone's faces, I can see what they're thinking. Exactly the same as me: *If I want to know what the weather's going to be like, Mr Stein, I'll look it up on the internet.*

I won't actually say it, of course. The brief flash of satisfaction wouldn't be worth being kept in during break or writing out lines or . . . So I just sit here and it feels like I'm literally melting with boredom. I really should concentrate, though. Exams are coming up in a couple of months' time, but I just can't seem to . . . My thoughts keep going back to Zehra. I can't get her out of my head. Between her and Alex, my brain's been taken hostage.

'. . . An air mass is an extremely large body of air whose properties of temperature and humidity, at any given altitude, are fairly similar in any horizontal direction . . .' Mr Stein drones on.

I'm making doodles in my textbook. Kelly whips around in the chair in front of me. She's holding up her Geography exercise book so I can see the picture she's drawn: a boy and a girl sitting up in a tree. Above the boy's head she's written *Alex* and above the girl's head is my name. Reaching forward, I try to grab the book from her, but she pulls it away quickly and makes a kissing action with her lips. I try to glare but instead I break into a smile.

She turns to the front again and looks at Mr Stein. My attention is back to the doodle in my book.

'Zeyneb?' I hear Mr Stein's voice and, by the level of irritation I detect in it, I can tell it's not the first time he's called me. Oops.

'Yes, sir?'

'Would you be so kind as to stop your reverie and write down your homework assignment?'

Are you forced to sign a contract to use words like *reverie* when you become a teacher? Or does he speak like that of his own free will?

'Yes, sir.' I pretend to write something down. I'll get it from Kelly later on.

At last the bell rings and we all scramble for the door. Alex is pushing past some of the others to get to me.

'Hey, Zeyneb,' he calls.

'Hey, Alex.' I nod, trying to seem cool. I am *not* going to go to pieces this time. I'll show him I'm just as normal as any other girl in our class.

'So, when do you want to get together?'

'Get together?' My bag slips right out of my hand on to the floor, and I almost trip over it. *What's he talking about?* 'What are you talking about?'

He picks up my bag and hands it back to me. 'For the project.'

'What project?' I sling the bag over my shoulder and start walking away from him.

'You weren't listening to a word he said, were you?'

'Who? Mr Stein? Er . . . maybe not. What did he say?'

I'm walking quickly now, searching the crowded corridor for Kelly, but Alex is keeping up. Different songs being played on MP3 players make a jumbled noise in the corridor, jumbling my thoughts.

Alex laughs. 'The homework project. We have to work in pairs and . . . well . . .'

I stop, looking up at him. 'And what?' But I already know what he's going to say.

'Mr Stein put the two of us together . . .'

'You and me?' I know my face has dropped. Of all the times I could be daydreaming in class, I had to choose today! Unbelievable. The day I get paired up with Alex.

He nods, and his eyes are sparkling.

'What . . . what about Kelly?' I try.

'She's with David.'

I pause, thinking it through. Maybe there's a way of

doing this alone. 'What do we have to do?'

'We have to research and write the project together, then present it to the class next Friday.'

So that's definitely teamwork, then.

'And he said we should get started as soon as possible,' Alex goes on. 'You want to come over to my house after school?'

I laugh, not a funny laugh like he just made a joke, more a you-must-be-out-of-your-mind laugh. 'Yeah, like my parents are going to allow that.'

He frowns. 'But it's for school,' he says, as if, for a single second, that would be a good enough excuse for me to go to a boy's house.

I sigh. I really don't want to have this conversation, don't want to explain to him what it's like to live inside *my* life. As soon as he finds out, as soon as he hears the details about my family, he'll stop looking at me in that way, stop asking me to go to the funfair, stop thinking I'm more than a seven-and-a-half. But there's no way around it.

'They won't let me go to your house, Alex. It just doesn't work that way. I'll speak to them tonight and see what they say and then I'll let you know. OK?'

He has no choice but to nod. I stare at him to see if his expression's changed, but he drops his head forward and lets his fringe hang over his face. Is he doing that on purpose? What's he trying to hide? What does he think about me now?

I put my mind firmly back on Geography. 'What's it

about, anyway?'

'What?' he asks.

'Our project?'

'I chose weather satellites.' He looks up again and he's grinning at me.

'You're kidding . . .'

We've reached our next class and we're filing through the door. Kelly appears at my side and she's got this goofy look on her face.

'Zeyneb and Alex, sitting in a tree,' she whispers, 'K.I.S.S.I.N.G. . . .'

'Very funny.' I force myself to smile at her but I know it's not convincing.

That night, when I sit down for supper with my parents and *Babaanne*, I can hardly eat. We're having red peppers stuffed with mince and rice, my favourite. But tonight, I'm just not hungry.

'*Baba, Anne*, I need to talk to you,' I say, and cringe as I hear the words come out of my mouth – the exact same words I used when I lied to go to Kelly's party. Are they going to believe me this time?

My parents look up. They can hear from the seriousness in my voice that I'm going to say something important, and that makes it even worse. Why can't I just be light and chatty about it? Why do I have to make it so hard before I even get started?

'There's this project we have to do for Geography, and we have to work in pairs,' I begin.

They stare at me expectantly.

'I have to work with one of the boys in my class, a boy called Alex.'

They nod. They're waiting. 'Well, it's kind of home-work. We can't do it in class and I . . . well, I . . . I'm not sure where we should do it . . .'

'Do it in one of the classrooms during break – with a teacher present,' *Anne* suggests. She looks chuffed, as if she's just solved all the world's problems.

'I can't. It's too much work to do during break. I . . . I mean, *we* have to do it after school.'

Baba just sits there quietly, listening. So far he hasn't said anything, hasn't asked a single question. He's just watching me. Does he believe me? Or has he somehow figured out that Alex is more than just an ordinary boy to me?

'Then do this homework of yours with Kelly. Why must it be with this boy?' my mum goes on.

'*Anne*, I can't get another partner. It doesn't work that way. We've all been paired up with boys. Kelly has to work with David.'

She pushes away her plate and folds her arms, looking at my father. 'What kind of school is this?'

I take a deep breath and get ready for another round of explaining, but my father stops me. Nodding, he speaks slowly: 'This is the way they do things here, Güler. We cannot ask Zeyneb to go against the stream. What will it do to her school marks if she is difficult about this?'

'It's true, *Anne*. There's really no other way of doing

this.' I'm so grateful he understands, I take hold of his hand and kiss the top of it. He strokes the back of my head.

I look up at him again. Now for the next difficult topic: 'Where should I say I'll meet up with this boy?'

I can see by the shock on their faces that they haven't yet considered the practical side of this issue. My mum takes a sip of water and spills it right down her front.

'The library?' I push on. It's best just to get this over with. 'Or here, at our house?'

I don't bother mentioning Alex's suggestion about getting together at his house. I'm not that stupid. But I'm hoping with all my might they'll agree to the library, so I don't have to drag him here, sit him down at our dining-room table, and spend the entire time crumpled up with embarrassment, like I'm dying inside, while my mother hovers around us.

They give me their answer.

After I've helped my mother with the dishes, I go to my bedroom to start my homework. Taking out my phone, I scroll through my contacts. One of them is listed simply as A. It's Alex's number. I saved it from that time after Kelly's party – another thing to add to my list of things I shouldn't do.

I send him a text: Hi Alex. We can get 2gether at my house after school 2mrw. Zeyneb.

And even though I'm all alone, I know my cheeks are bright red. I pinch my eyes shut in anticipation of the embarrassment that is bound to follow and press *Send*. Well, at least now I know he'll stop liking me. But I can't help wondering what he'll be thinking as he reads it.

12

OK. Here we go – more problems. More rapids and waterfalls, more crocodiles and sharks. I wish I could go and lie under my hydrangea, but there isn't time.

Shark-problem number one: after school today the most handsome boy in my class is coming to my house. Yes, *today*. Actually, in about thirty minutes.

Shark-problem number two: my mum is about to faint at the mere idea of a boy and a girl alone in the same room. This morning she slid my fried egg into my glass of tea instead of on to my plate and I just know it was because she was imagining this boy who'd be coming into her home.

Shark-problem number three: Alex and I have to study weather satellites. Probably – no, definitely – the most boring subject ever invented.

I am a total mess.

I can't concentrate on a thing in class because of all the thoughts rushing through my head – like a waterfall, or a rapid, or both together . . . Will *Anne* actually sit down at the table too? Or insist that there's at least so much space between us? Or, total horror, arrange for one of my cousins to be a chaperone and sit with us the whole time?

Each time I play the scene out in my head it gets worse. Staring at the clock on the wall, I try making the hands stand still by means of telepathy. Yes, I know – it doesn't work. At last I hear that dreaded final bell of the day. My heart is in the bottom of my shoes as I make my slow, slow way over to the bicycle shed. Alex has gone ahead and is waiting for me.

I see him standing there, leaning against his bike. His jet-black fringe flops over one eye. He stares at me as I approach. Does he wink at me or am I imagining it? The anxiety I've been feeling all day evaporates and I feel a flutter of excitement. *Stop it, Zeyneb!* I tell myself.

Get a grip. Nothing can happen here. Talk to him like you talk to Kelly. But I know I have to warn him what our house is like before he gets there. What am I going to say?

'Hey, Zey,' he says, smiling. 'Ready to go?'

Probably the last time he'll ever call me *Zey* after he hears what I've got to say. I take a deep breath.

'Have you been to a Turkish person's house before?' I ask.

'Yep, sure – I go over to Mustafa's place all the time,' he says.

Another deep breath. 'And . . . does he have any sisters?'

Alex looks surprised. 'He's got two. One older and one younger.'

93

'Have you ever been alone in the same room with either of them?'

'Why're you asking me all this?' he wants to know, his forehead creased and his dimple nowhere in sight.

'Have you?'

He's quiet for a moment while he thinks about my question. 'No, I don't think so,' he says at last.

Thank goodness for Mustafa. 'Well, that's how it is with us too, Alex.'

'How is what with you? What are you talking about?'

I swear, I'd be prepared to get zero for this stupid project if I could walk away from this right now. But it wouldn't be fair to Alex. I push on: 'Boys and girls our age, well, they . . . they . . . Just expect my mum to be around us a lot, OK?'

I've done it – the most embarrassing conversation I've had with a boy. Ever.

Alex nods. 'Sure, no problem. My mum's a housewife too.'

He has absolutely no idea what I'm talking about, but I'm through explaining. I don't have a single gram of courage left any more. He's just going to have to see it with his own eyes.

We jump on our bikes and start pedalling home fast. I'm in front, going like the wind; one minute I'm hoping like mad he won't catch up with me and the next wishing he would, because I can't think of anything I'd rather be doing than cycling at his side, talking. Eventually we get home, and, yes, I'm still slightly ahead of him. The torturous journey is over; now for the worst part.

I wonder what his house looks like. Like ours, or is it much fancier? Do they have a gardener? Is Alex the kind of boy who would notice a garden? Probably not, I decide, not many people pay attention to things like that. Pity, because our house looks kind of nice from the outside. I see the hydrangea bush with its huge leaves just peeping out from the wall. What I wouldn't give to crawl under there right now! I take a big gulp of air and we head up the front steps.

I'm about to tell him to take off his shoes, then see he's already done it and is putting on a pair of slip-ons to go inside. He goes straight for the guest slip-ons, the less worn, smarter ones. It's obvious that Mustafa has explained all of this to him. I'm so unbelievably grateful to Mustafa for saving me from having to explain the shoe situation I decide to buy him a Coke tomorrow from the tuck shop.

We walk into the hallway and I can only think about one thing – please let *Anne* not be wearing that awful apron of hers, the faded green one covered in little white flowers that must be at least fifty years old. Will he notice? And what about the huge gold-framed mirror in the dining room? I've only seen ones like that in other Turkish homes. Or the vase with peacock feathers sticking out of it instead of flowers. I'm going over every detail in our house, every piece of furniture, wondering if there's a single thing that will seem normal.

I'm about to yell casually, '*Anne*, I'm home,' hoping to

sound like any other teenager, but instead I bump straight into her and, yes, she's got the apron on and is wringing her dishcloth. Great.

It's like she's been waiting just behind the front door for us.

With my final shred of dignity I hope that Alex doesn't notice me blushing. Yet again.

'Hello, *Anne*,' I say and plant a kiss on her cheek. I'd love to skip the kiss but I'm petrified she'll say something, or worse, *make* me give her one, like a little kid. She has absolutely no concept of 'embarrassing'.

'How was school?' she asks mechanically, but her eyes aren't on me at all. No, they're fixed on this very strange specimen I've dragged into our house: an unaccompanied teenage boy.

'This is Alex.' I do my best to sound casual, as if this is just a regular boy from my class and not the one who sends my heart into a spin. That would be all I need, for *Anne* to suspect I feel something for him!

My mum nods and stretches out her hand for a handshake. 'Welcome to our home,' she says.

Why does she have to be so formal? I bend down and pretend to adjust my sock just so I can stop watching this.

'Hey, Mrs . . . Mrs Ozturk.' Alex flashes his grin at her, the dimple popping.

There's no way you're going to win her over that easily, I think, but I'm grateful to him for trying.

'Where's *Babaanne*?' I ask.

'At the allotment with your father,' says my mum, and

I'm relieved. Just *Anne* to deal with – that's something at least. How much worse would it be if there were three grown-ups here instead of one? *Baba* would start cross-examining him about what his parents did for a living, and *Babaanne*, well, you could never tell with her . . .

'Leave your bags in the dining room, Zeyneb.' My mum's turned all practical. Wringing the eternal dish-cloth in her hands, she heads towards the kitchen. 'You can do your homework in there after you've eaten.'

Without even a glance at Alex – I don't dare – I dump my bag and follow her. I hear his footsteps behind me.

'Actually, Mrs Ozturk,' Alex pipes up, 'I'm not really hungry. Maybe just a . . .'

But he doesn't get to finish his sentence because my mum whips round and fixes a strained smile on him. I know exactly what she's thinking: he doesn't know the first thing about being a gracious guest.

'Nonsense,' she says, her smile still strained, 'you can't do your schoolwork on an empty stomach. Your brain needs food too, you know. I'm sure there will be something you like.'

I want to kick myself. I should've warned Alex about this too. I should've told him there was no way he was going to come to our house for the first time and not be overwhelmed by our famous hospitality.

And then, as I walk into the kitchen, I almost let out the loudest, groaniest groan of my life.

From the amount of food *Anne*'s laid out on the table it would seem our brains have been living in some famine-stricken country. A feast for at least six people is spread before us. What I wouldn't give to see two simple sandwiches and a glass of milk, but of course I should've known that would've been as probable as me becoming prime minister.

'Whoah,' Alex exclaims. He peers at the plate of cigar-shaped stuffed vine leaves. '*Sarmas*. D'you make these yourself?'

My mum nods. I can see a smile about to break out on her lips.

'My gran makes them too. They're my favourite,' he says, and my gratitude towards him nearly overwhelms me.

'Your grandmother is Turkish?'

'She's Greek.'

The smile disappears again. I sigh – this is going to be one long afternoon.

We wash our hands and sit down, helping ourselves to small portions of the many dishes arranged before us. My mum pours us each a glass of tea. Has he ever had Turkish tea? Does Mustafa's mum also serve it to him when he's there? Will he like it? I watch tentatively from the corner of my eye as Alex pops a *sarma* into his mouth.

'Man, these are even better than my gran's,' he says.

I don't know if he's saying this because it's true or because he wants to make a good impression on my mum, but, whatever the reason, it's worked, because I see the faint flutter of a smile back on her lips.

At last we finish eating. We're stuffed to bursting point because my mum has hovered over us the whole time, insisting we try each of the dishes she's prepared. The last thing I feel like doing now is sitting down to work on the stupid weather project, but there's no way I can suggest to *Anne* that we catch a breath of fresh air in the garden first. We head into the dining room with its white table and chairs, oversized gold-rimmed vases with fake white roses, and a verse from the Koran painted in gold Arabic letters on one of the walls.

'Shall we sit down?' I say.

As soon as he's taken a seat, I sit down directly opposite him. I hear my mum in the kitchen, tidying up.

'You want some biscuits?' she calls.

Alex and I look at each other and burst out laughing.

'I couldn't eat another thing!' he whispers. 'Help me . . .'

'No, thanks, *Anne*,' I call back.

And so our first homework session starts. Even though I couldn't care less about weather satellites, Alex seems to like them and he makes me just a bit more interested.

We work hard and get a lot done simply from complete embarrassment, and because there's no chance of us relaxing for even a millisecond. My mum fusses around in the kitchen and every five minutes or so she makes a dash into the dining room on the pretence of fetching something or putting something away. I swear she's washed every plate in our house at least six times and returned them to the sideboard one by one. I don't know what to do: I can't give *Anne* a pleading look to ask her to

99

stop, because that'll just convince her there's something going on that shouldn't be. I also can't just sit here and let Alex think this hovering mum situation is normal.

'She's not always like this,' I whisper when I hear her in the kitchen.

'What's wrong?' he asks.

I flash him a weak smile. 'It's like I told you. It's the boy–girl thing.'

He nods and looks back down at his library book. Is it an understanding nod? Is it a this-girl's-crazy nod? I just can't tell. I look at my own book and hope with all my heart that the afternoon will be over quickly.

After about two hours we decide we've done enough and Alex says he has to get home. He says goodbye to *Anne*, all stiff and polite, and I walk him out to his bike.

There's nothing I can say now. He's seen what he's seen and I'm sure he's wishing his head off that he'd been given another Geography partner. I bet he doesn't even like me any more. I know that's what I wanted, but still . . . it makes me feel . . . it makes me feel sad. There's nothing I can do about it.

'She's nice, your mum,' he says.

I want to tell him he doesn't have to lie for the sake of politeness – that I know as well as he does how unbearable she was this afternoon – but I can't. Not without insulting her.

'Thanks.' I smile, but it's an automatic smile. I'm already picturing him giving everyone in our class a frame-by-frame picture of my home life.

'Don't say . . .' I try. 'In class tomorrow, don't . . . please . . .'

Alex stops at the gate, his hand on his bike. 'Don't what?'

'Don't make fun of her,' I say. My voice is so quiet even I can hardly hear it.

His eyes widen and he takes a step back towards me. We're so close our hands touch. I step back, my hand jerking as if I've been burned, and glance quickly at our front window. The lace curtain isn't moving though.

'I've had a nice time,' he says. 'Why would I do that?'

I shrug. I can't even look him in the eye. I reach out and touch his bicycle seat just so I have something to do.

'Well, I won't. OK? D'you believe me?

Instead of touching this stupid bike, I wish I could let my fingers brush over his again, but of course I can't.

'Thanks, Alex.'

'No problem.'

Then he jumps on his bike and rides off, literally, into the sunset – the sun really is setting, the whole sky is pink and orange and red, and there he goes, pedalling off. Like a knight in a fairy tale – except he's on a bike instead of a white horse.

13

Why didn't I beg my mum to take me shopping for my own dress after Kelly's party? Why did I trust her to get me something halfway decent? Why am I so stupid? Why, why, why?

I have another huge shark-problem – and this time I have no one to blame but myself.

Saturday afternoon and I'm standing in front of the mirror in my mother's bedroom, frozen stiff and wearing the pale-blue dress my mum bought me for my cousin's wedding – which is tonight.

It is the least flattering thing I have worn in my whole life. Ever. I can't believe I have to leave the house looking like this.

The girl in the mirror looks like a pruned apple tree – long, skinny branches with big, knobbly nodes all over the place. My shoulders, my elbows (luckily my knees are covered) have never looked so bony and so sticky-outy in my life in these sleeves, and the bits of arms and legs in between are far too long and far too thin. My chest is like the door to *Baba*'s shed. Well, to be honest, it's always been flat, but this dress just makes it so much more noticeable. My hair is piled on top of my head in some type of weird birds' nest.

'*Anne*, I can't go like this,' I wail. 'I look awful.'

'Nonsense. You look lovely,' she says, and goes on fussing with her own dress – a sparkly light-green thing, narrow at the waist, with these long lacy sleeves. 'Go to Elif in the other room and ask her to put on some mascara for you.'

Oh yes, a bit of mascara's going to do the trick. It will definitely transform me from Disney-princess-gone-wrong into a supermodel.

I roll my eyes and – oops – she sees me. She's watching me from the mirror propped up on the bed, hairpins pinched between her lips. She glares at me as she slides them deftly one by one over the edges of her headscarf to secure it. Giving it a few light tugs, she makes sure it's not going anywhere, then holds the remaining pins out towards me.

'Do you want me to do it?'

'Do what?'

'Pin your headscarf on for you?'

'My . . . my . . .'

The wedding energy that's been buzzing round the room, round the whole house today, kind of quietens down and I feel another type of tension creeping in. My mum feels it too. Her face has turned all serious. I stare at her because I don't know what to say.

'I thought you loved it?' she says. 'The headscarf I bought for you . . .'

'I do, *Anne*. I told you, it's beautiful.'

'So what's the problem?'

What's the problem? *What's the problem?*

I want to shout at her: the problem is that Elif says it's not what you wear that makes you a modern woman, but Kelly says the exact opposite. She says people will assume I can't think for myself, that I'm radical. The problem is that I have no idea what kind of gazelle I am – a headscarf-wearing gazelle or a sweeter-greener-grass gazelle.

But I don't say any of these things to her.

In the next room I hear Dilara give a little shriek and I love my two-year-old niece more than ever for giving me an escape route.

'I'm going to see if I can help with the little ones,' I mutter, and rush from the room.

All this wedding madness is making me crazy. And we're just the cousins! I can't imagine what Ebrar, the bride, must be feeling. I don't know if she's into all this fussing and over-the-topness. I can't imagine how anyone could be. I don't think I'm ever going to get married. I'll probably fall down dead just from the shopping and getting ready. No, I really need to get away from this for a while. I don't go to help Elif.

In the lounge I find my father perched uncomfortably on the edge of the sofa in his suit and tie. He looks up at me.

'Zeyneb?' His eyes are glistening. 'You look beautiful, *kizim*.'

I smile because I'm grateful for his lie. 'You look good too, *Baba*.'

He shoves his fingers into his collar and starts tugging at it. 'You know how I hate to get dressed up like this.'

'Me too,' I say.

'Two peas in a pod, that's what we are.'

'Except you get to wear trousers and I have to wear this stupid dress.'

'Tomorrow we'll both put on our old clothes and go to the allotment, all right?'

'Deal.'

Flashing him a smile, I walk through to the garden, picking up my phone from the sideboard as I go.

'Where are you going?' he calls.

'Outside for five minutes. I need a breath of fresh air.'

He's the one person who can understand this in the midst of all this madness.

I long to crawl into my secret corner under the hydrangea bush, but the potential for a hissy-fit from my mum if I mess up my outfit simply isn't worth it, so I plonk myself down on one of the garden chairs instead.

It's twilight and the heat of the day is quickly leaking away. My sleeves are so thin I'm covered in goosebumps.

I scroll through the contacts on my phone. There's something I need to do – someone I need to call. I've been thinking about it for days, and now is the moment.

I've finally found the courage.

I find the number I saved on my phone and press *Call*.

I wait. Several long rings. I wait. Suddenly I hear a click and it goes over to voicemail: 'Hi, you've reached Zehra's phone. To schedule an appointment you can phone me from Monday to Friday between 9 a.m. and 5 p.m. Leave a message and I'll get back to you.'

I push the cancel button and sit staring at the useless phone in my hand. Stupid Zeyneb. I should've known. People don't work twenty-four hours a day. And what was I going to say to her anyway?

But I've made up my mind to do this now. I'll leave a message. I push *Redial*, hear the long rings and wait for it to go over to voicemail again.

Except it doesn't.

'Hello?'

'Um . . . um . . . um . . .'

'Hello? Is anyone there?'

'Yes, yes, I'm here. It's me, Zeyneb.'

'Zeyneb?'

'Am I speaking to Zehra?'

'You are.' Her words are slower now, more cautious. Obviously she's thinking I'm some kind of nut.

'You came to our school last week.'

'Oh, yes, that's right. And you've got some more questions for me about university?'

'No.'

'No?'

'I'm too young. I can't go yet.'

106

'OK, so why are you—'

'I mean, I want to go later, when I finish school, I told you that already, and Mr Rubens, that's my Maths teacher, he says I'm smart enough, but it's just that . . . it's just that . . .'

I hear her breathing at the other end. She's waiting for me to say something. How stupid can I be? Phoning this woman on the evening of my cousin's wedding.

'I'm sorry,' I say at last.

'It's all right. You've obviously got a question for me. Why don't you slow down, take your time, and tell me what it is?'

'I . . . I don't know if I should wear a headscarf,' I blurt out.

'A headscarf? I see. Well, what do your parents—'

'I'm clever, you see, and I didn't really ask to be clever, I just am. Not that I'm ungrateful or anything. Not that I'd rather be stupid, it's just that . . . Well, I've got this gift and I know I have to do something with it. I *want* to do something with it. I want to go to university and study Botany like you said, and make my parents proud, but I just don't know if wearing a headscarf is going to stand in my way . . .'

And then I take a breath.

'OK,' she says slowly, and I picture her nodding. 'You know, I get asked this question more times than you'd imagine.'

'You do?' My body gives a little shiver. It's partly from the cold but also from relief. I'm so glad – so glad! – to hear I'm not the only girl with this question on my mind.

'Yes.'

'So what do you say?'

'I say that the headscarf's not the issue. It's how strong you are inside that's important. Do you have what it takes to study at university level for three or four years? Do you have what it takes to be a minority at university and still try to fit in? Do you have what it takes to spend half your time in your own culture and the other half in another culture without losing sight of who you are? If you think you can do these things, Zeyneb, if you think you have what it takes, then you'll be OK. Headscarf or no headscarf.'

'Thanks, but . . . but . . .'

'But what?'

'That doesn't help me now. Tonight!' I wail.

'You don't have to decide tonight. Take your time and think carefully about it.'

'You don't understand, they're all upstairs getting ready for the wedding and they want me to put on a headscarf. Tonight!'

She's laughing gently. 'Then go upstairs and put it on. Just for tonight. At the very least you'll know what it feels like. It doesn't mean you have to wear it again tomorrow, does it?'

She's right. Somehow what she's saying makes sense. It doesn't mean I have to wear it again tomorrow. I realize I'm grinning, congratulating myself that I had the insight to phone her.

'Thank you,' I say.

'It's a pleasure.'

'No, I really mean it. *Thank you.*'

She laughs again at the other end. 'C'mon. Off you go. Go get ready for the wedding.'

I go back to *Anne*'s bedroom. She's sitting on the edge of her bed slipping on her new shoes. I hand her my headscarf.

'Can you put it in your handbag and take it with you?' I ask.

'But I . . .' She crinkles her nose and raises her eyebrows.

'I can always decide later, can't I?' I tell her.

Anne lets out a long sigh. 'I suppose you can, *kizim*. I suppose you can.'

14

So we're at the wedding, or, should I say, the feast. Ebrar and her husband, Murat, had the civil service yesterday, signing all the documents and stuff to make them officially husband and wife. And then, this afternoon, while we were all getting ready, the *hodja*, a spiritual leader, went to Ebrar's house and did the religious part of the ceremony. The only people who are there are the bride and groom (obviously), my *teyze* and her husband, and Murat's parents and their witnesses. Only then was Ebrar allowed to come to the feast. Her younger brother, Ahmed, would have tied a red ribbon around her waist to show she was pure and then she would have had to say her goodbyes to her family. But all of that was done in a small group. There's never a lot of people present.

I'm sitting here now at the wedding feast, tucked away at a table in the corner. Dinner has been served. Silvan and Dilara are in the room next door, where they have special entertainment for the kids. My cousins are either on the dance floor or walking round with their friends discussing everyone's outfits. *Teyze* is strutting like a peacock while my cousin Semra hovers at her side, acting like a grown-up even though she's only eleven.

My mum and Elif are dancing, their arms locked around the shoulders of their neighbours, a ring of a dozen women spinning faster and faster as the music gets more frenzied. My mum's kicking up her feet, her back arched, her new dress shimmering – there's no frumpy apron or dishcloth tonight. And Elif, with her tall elegant figure and long black hair – well, she must be one of the most beautiful women here.

Babaanne hasn't joined the group of dancers but she's there, at the edge of the dance floor, leaning heavily on her walking stick, making miniature dance moves with her feet and shoulders. Anyone can tell she used to look like Elif when she was young. She motions to me to go and join them. I shake my head and she frowns.

I'm not much of a dancer. I don't have the same natural grace as *Anne* or Elif, but I don't want to disappoint *Babaanne* and I do know the steps to this dance. I know the steps to all the dances – I've been dancing them since I was a little kid. And it's better than sitting here, slumped at the table.

Walking past *Babaanne* to get to the dance floor, she gives me a little nudge. I smile at her and speed up my steps to get in time with the fast-moving circle of women. Elif sees me and immediately lets go of her neighbour's shoulder so I can hook in with her. Off we go, faster and faster, laughing, kicking up our legs, intricate steps, first forward and then back, twelve women temporarily become one dancing mass.

My headscarf slips off my shoulders (which is where I've been wearing it for the last hour-and-a-half instead of on my head). It falls to the floor and we're moving too fast for me to let go and pick it up but, from the corner of my eye, I see *Babaanne* poke at it with her walking stick and pull it towards her at the edge of the dance floor.

I wouldn't say the headscarf-wearing experiment has been a huge success tonight. I allowed *Anne* to pin it to my head when we first got here. Then I had to spend the whole night listening to everyone's comments:

'Oh, Zeyneb, I didn't know you were wearing a *hijab* now!'

'Your parents must be so proud . . .'

'Such a respectful daughter, Zeyneb . . .'

'Is this for good now? Are you going to be wearing it all the time?'

Can't you just mind your own business? I wanted to say. It made me feel cross and self-conscious, so I took it off and draped it over my shoulders like a kind of shawl. Anyway, it hid my bony bits better than my sleeves did. *Babaanne* said you felt protected when you wore a head-scarf, but I haven't felt protected tonight. All it's done is draw attention to me, attention I don't want.

The song ends and another one starts up. I stay. I dance again. I laugh. I've forgotten how much fun this can be. Another three songs and then I decide to go back to my seat. I want to catch my breath, have a drink of water. Soon the men will go on to the dance floor and after that the master of ceremonies will call on the guests to start pinning money on the bride's dress, to hand over gifts of gold jewellery or envelopes of cash.

At the table I scratch in *Anne*'s handbag to find my phone. I'll go outside for a bit of fresh air, maybe give Kelly a call so she can make me laugh. She's good at that. I make my way towards the door.

'Where are you going?' I hear my father's voice as he steps out from a throng of men standing by the dance floor.

'I'm just going outside for a little while.'

'With whom?' he asks.

'Alone.' I shrug.

'Do you want me to come with you?'

I shake my head. 'I'll be fine.'

'You want my jacket? It's cold outside.'

'No, thanks, *Baba*.'

He nods and lets me go.

Outside I lean against the side of the building so no one will notice me. Staring up the silver slipper of the moon, I wonder what Alex is doing tonight.

There's a group of boys huddled together, smoking and laughing loudly, doing their very best to impress the four young women standing a little way away. One of them is smoking herself. If any of the elders sees her, or if one of the young ones tells on her, she'll be in big trouble. They're giggling and batting their heavily-made-up eyelids. Within the next six months we'll be standing here again, I predict, for another wedding. One of theirs.

After a while they go back in and I'm left alone, except for the odd smoker who rushes out into the cold for a few furious draws on a cigarette. I take my mobile, scroll down to Kelly's number and push *Call*. Immediately it goes over to voicemail. Strange: her phone's always on, but then I remember she's gone to the cinema with her mum tonight.

Then all of a sudden the phone gives a shrill ring in my hand. Startled, without looking at the screen, I press *Accept* and hold it to my ear.

'Kelly?'

'No, it's me, Alex.'

His voice makes me feel dizzy. I have no idea what to say to him.

'Zeyneb? You still there?'

'I'm here.'

'What are you doing?'

'I'm at a wedding. My cousin got married today. And you?'

'At home, in my room, watching TV. I thought I'd phone you . . .'

In spite of myself, I laugh. 'Obviously.'

Of course I know I shouldn't be standing here talking to Alex, the moon shining away above me. It's all far too romantic. But I'm sick and tired of always trying to be good, trying to please everyone, listening to all the stupid comments about my headscarf. I just want to do what I want to do.

'Look . . .' He sounds hesitant. 'I . . . I just wanted to say, I had fun at your house this week.'

'Really?' I can't quite believe that. 'We weren't exactly there to have fun.' I smile. 'Unless you really do like weather satellites . . .'

I hear him laugh. 'But I did. I mean, not the weather satellites. I had fun being with you . . . just . . . well, it's fun for me.'

I have to lean back against the cold wall so my knees don't buckle underneath me. *He likes being with me – even after meeting* Anne!

'I mean, even if we don't . . . if we're not allowed . . . you know, like the thing you said about your parents being all strict . . . even if we're just friends, it's OK with me.'

My eyes are shut and I'm biting hard on my bottom lip. I can't believe he just said that. Can't believe anyone has ever uttered such a beautiful sentence before. It feels as if I'm about to take off and fly to the moon.

'Zeyneb?'

'I'm still here,' I say softly.

'What do you think?'

'About what?'

'What I just said.'

'I think . . . I'm not allowed to . . . like a boy in that way, Alex.' I'm almost whispering.

'I know . . .' I can tell he's struggling too. 'But the part about being friends?'

'It's a good part,' I say. 'Friends is good.'

'Friends is good,' he repeats.

I'm too busy grinning to myself like an idiot to answer him.

'So I'll come round next week to work on our project?'

I nod before I realize he can't see me nodding. *Dork!* 'Yes, sure.'

He pauses again. 'And then . . . how about the funfair next weekend? To celebrate the end of our project. You want to come with me?'

'You just said—'

'Not alone,' he adds quickly. 'I'll ask some of my friends, you ask Kelly, and then we can go in a group.'

I know exactly what I should say to his suggestion. There's no question in my mind about it. I know how I feel about him, and I'm pretty sure he feels the same way, and there's nothing *just friends* about it. We'd be going in a group but I'd be *with* him. It would be a date, wouldn't it?

He's saying all the right things – but they're not true. Not really.

I picture *Baba* and *Anne* and Elif and *Babaanne* standing next to me, their arms crossed, glaring at me. They're waiting for me to give the right answer to Alex's question.

'I have to ask my parents.' It's not really the right answer – but it's not wrong either.

The door opens. Someone is coming outside. It's my father. His eyes are scanning the car park in search of me.

'I've got to go,' I whisper urgently and end the call. I hold the phone guiltily behind my back.

'Ah, Zeyneb, there you are,' *Baba* says, and his eyes

light up. 'You've got the right idea. Far too hot and crowded inside.' He's standing next to me and he starts taking off his jacket. 'Look at you, you must be freezing in this dress.'

'I'm fine, *Baba*,' I say, even though I'm not. I'm not fine at all.

15

Alex comes round on Monday after school. I haven't dared look at him all day – all I can hear is his voice in my head saying, *'I had fun being with you . . .'*

It's one of those warm April afternoons when actually it's madness to be sitting indoors in our stuffy old dining room.

'Weird to be studying weather inside,' Alex says, reading my mind, as *Anne* fusses around, dusting the doorframe. She's almost run out of chores to do in here.

Outside the daffodils are basking in the sun and the blue tits are collecting grass and lint and hair for their nests. It's true – I'd love to be outside too. But I dare not suggest it to *Anne*. No, no, no! That would be like saying I wanted to be alone with him and I'd have a fainting mum on my hands. So, as a kind of compromise, I resolve to do my maths outside after Alex has gone home.

OK. So we're sitting here, I've got our diagram of a satellite orbiting the earth in front of me, and Alex has a library book open on the table.

'What's this thing called? This one here?' I ask, pointing at a long protrusion from the side of the satellite.

Alex says nothing. I look up, but he's not looking at the diagram. He's looking at me, his chin resting on his hand.

'Alex?' I say.

'Oh, sorry. What?' His elbow slips off the edge of the table.

I laugh. 'What's this thing called? I need to label it.'

'It's a . . . it's a . . .' But then he laughs too. 'I'm sorry, Zeyneb, I have no idea what it's called.'

From the kitchen we hear the sound of *Anne*'s phone ringing. When she picks up I hear panic in her voice and I know something's wrong. Alex and I look at each other. He's heard it too. Next thing we know, she's standing in the dining room, a stricken look on her face, wringing her dishcloth.

'Elif just called,' she cries. 'Dilara's fallen on the stairs and she has a cut above her eye. She wants me to go over and watch Silvan while she takes her to get stitches.' My mum is saying all of this in Turkish, a clear sign of how distressed she is.

Poor Dilara! I drop my pen and stand up. 'I'll come with you.'

The dishcloth is getting extra wringing now. 'No, Zeyneb, you can't. *Babaanne*'s gone for a walk and someone has to be here when she gets back because she doesn't have a key.'

'But *Anne*—' I try to argue.

'When your father gets home you can get on your bike and come over to Elif's place, all right?'

We both watch as my mum takes off her apron and abandons it on the back of a chair. She's got the car keys in her hand and she's halfway out the door when she turns to me: 'You let the boy out now. He can come back another time.' And with that, she's gone.

Alex is looking puzzled. 'What just happened?'

So I give him the details. While I'm doing the whole explanation about the emergency, I'm tempted to leave out my mum's last words. I mean, I know it's madness, but we're here, alone in the house, hovering-mum out of sight, for this one and only time and . . . Just five minutes! What could we possible do wrong in five minutes? But . . . what about Dilara? Is she going to be OK? Should I even be having these thoughts while Elif speeds across town to the hospital with my two-year-old niece?

He said he just wanted to be friends and I believe him. I *want* to believe him. And then again, I don't. *I had fun being with you* . . . The only thing I know for sure is that I don't want him to go home. But I'm strict with myself. I remember my promise not to lie to my parents and I think about the fact that my mum trusts me. Eventually I force the words out, though it really hurts.

'My mum says you have to go home now, Alex. I'm sorry. I—'

'But can't we . . . shouldn't we at least try to finish . . .'

I shake my head. Slowly. I wish – how I wish! – I could give him a different answer.

'OK, it's cool. I understand,' he says, and he's trying really hard to make his voice sound convincing, but it doesn't, and I hear what's beneath it: disappointment.

Of course I don't want him to be disappointed, but . . . well, imagine how I'd feel if he was *pleased* to get out of here, happy to get away from me and my strange family . . . That would be worse, wouldn't it?

'I can give you something to drink before you leave?' I offer tentatively. *It's because it's so warm outside and he's got to cycle all the way home . . . it would be rude to let him go home without offering him anything . . . my parents have always taught me to be hospitable . . .* This is what I tell myself, but I know it's a lie. The reason I'm offering Alex a drink has got nothing to do with politeness or good manners.

He nods and I practically sprint to the kitchen to find us something to drink, something that, for once, is not tea. I bet at his house they drink Coke and Fanta and Sprite all the time. We only get that on special occasions. Finding a carton of fruit juice, I pour out two glasses and throw in some ice cubes for extra sophistication.

Back in the dining room, the drinks in my hands, I see Alex has packed up his books.

I hand him his apple juice, and before I can think it through, I've said it: 'Do you want to see the garden?'

'The garden?'

I nod. 'It's kind of like a hobby of mine. You know, plants and stuff.' I bite my lip, wondering what his reaction will be.

'Sure,' he says. 'I like plants.'

He follows me outside. I give him a little tour, stopping at key places to give him the explanations. Key places to me, at least, because this garden has been an important piece of my life since I was a baby. I show him the eight slender yellow heads on my Fire Flame tulips, Turkish flowers that I've managed to coax into bloom; the spot where I fell out of the tree when I was little and broke my collar bone; the rose bush, the one with the white buds, which we planted when Dilara was born . . . Alex is probably bored senseless but I can't stop myself. I just keep on rambling.

'This is where I buried my hamster last year,' I say, standing in front of a little patch of crocuses.

'I've never known a girl who was so into her garden,' he says.

Is that a good thing? Should I be more into music and film stars? He's probably thinking what a dork I am.

'Well,' I say, turning my back on the crocuses, 'I like other things too, you know. I mean, things like Facebook and MTV and stuff.'

But it's as if he's not listening. He's just staring at me. 'That's what I like about you,' he says quietly. 'You're not like the other girls. You're not always talking about boys and make-up and clothes . . .'

He takes a step closer to me and the fingers of his hand touch my fingers, like they did the last time he left my house.

I know I should step back. Pull my hand away at the

very least. I know I shouldn't be standing here like this, but I'm stuck. I literally can't move from this spot. Can't even open my mouth. I can only stare straight back at him, focus on the tiny flecks of yellow in his irises. Have they always been there? He's bending his neck and his face is coming closer to mine. I know what's coming.

I want to run away.

I want to scream.

But I do nothing.

I feel the warm air from his nose on my cheek. I smell the faint scent of school books on him. I know I'm breathing too quickly. His lips are slightly parted and I'm looking at them. And then they're on mine. His lips. They're warm, soft. And they're sending me flying through space along with the weather satellites.

Now I know that I really must stop this. Stop it right now. There's no way I should be feeling like this. No way I should be anywhere near weather satellites. But stopping it is the hardest thing I've ever had to do in my whole life. All I want to do is step closer to him, let him put his arms around me . . .

But I don't. I jump back and turn my head away from him.

'I think . . .' I'm struggling for breath, can only mumble. 'I think you need to go home now.'

'I'm sorry,' he says, but he doesn't look it. 'I just . . . I like you, Zeyneb . . .'

'There's nothing . . . you don't have to be . . .' I'm having enormous trouble talking, like I'm just learning to speak this very second. There are other sentences getting in the way of the ones that are supposed to come out. Sentences like: *Don't go. Let your fingers touch mine. Kiss me again.*

But at last the right sentences win: 'You don't have to be sorry, Alex. You just have to go home now.'

I find the courage to look at him and he nods. He understands. He doesn't have to say goodbye because I can read it in his eyes. I don't have to say, 'I'm not going to see you out. I'm going to stay right here,' because he understands this too.

Then he's crossing the lawn towards the house. My eyes follow him. Just before he reaches the back porch I see him jolt, his back stiffening, and he stares up at the top floor of our house.

I follow his gaze.

Babaanne is standing at her bedroom window, looking out over the back garden.

16

Now there are a couple of things I'm sure about: 100 per cent sure. No, 200 per cent for that matter. Forget about sharks. These are crocodiles. Huge green crocodiles that haven't eaten anything for weeks, lying on the river bank of my life, their mouths gaping open.

Crocodile number one: no matter how open-minded *Babaanne* is, no matter how much gazelle-in-search-of-greener-grass she is, there's no way, *no way* that she can accept a boy kissing me at home when my parents are away.

Crocodile number two: there is also no way she will let it slide and not discuss with my dad what she saw us doing.

Crocodile number three: my parents' reaction, when they found out I lied to them about Kelly's party, was nothing, absolutely *nothing*, compared to what it will be if they find out about this.

OK. Those are the things I'm sure about. And there's only one thing I'm not sure about, but this one thing is *very important* for my decision about what to do next. I'll call it a crocodile-catcher:

I have no idea whether *Babaanne* actually saw us kissing or not.

It's the next day. No bomb has exploded at our house, but I know that doesn't mean a thing. *Babaanne* is going to let me sweat this out, let me wonder whether in fact she did see me or didn't, let me dwell in uncertainty, suffer in remorse. In other words, she's a world champion in the number-one hobby for adults: letting you think about what you've done.

And I am. I'm thinking and I'm thinking and I'm sorry and I realize I was wrong. I hardly slept at all last night. I don't see her at breakfast this morning. Sneaking into the kitchen when I hear her go to the bathroom (luckily she spends *ages* in the bathroom!), I gobble down my breakfast at record speed. I give *Baba* and *Anne* a kiss and realize this might very well be the last moment of peace in this house for absolutely ages, probably the rest of my life.

I grab my school bag, jump on my bike and I'm off towards Kelly's place. What will *Babaanne* tell them when she gets out of the bathroom?

'What's wrong?' Kelly demands as soon as she sees me.

'What do you mean?' It's hard to actually put into words what happened, even to her.

'I can see something's wrong,' she says. 'What's happened?'

126

Taking a deep breath, I force myself to say it. 'Alex kissed me yesterday at my house.' I can see she wants to smile. The corners of her mouth are twitching. 'Don't you dare smile!' I say. 'This is serious.'

'And that's what's wrong?' she asks. 'A kiss?'

'Kelly!'

'What was it like?'

I groan. 'Please just pay attention! I need to tell you what happened. When we were finished, you know, after the kiss and stuff, we looked up and saw *Babaanne* standing at her bedroom window.'

'Oh!' Kelly knows enough to know this is a Big Problem.

'I don't know if she saw us or not but, if she did, I'm dead.'

'What'll they do?'

'Take me out of school for starters. Probably shove me into some all-girls' school.'

'They can't do that,' she gasps.

'Oh yes, they can,' I say, 'and that's only the beginning.'

'You can run away. You can come live with us.'

'Yeah, sure, like they won't know where to find me.'

'But they can't just take you away like that,' she says.

I don't answer her because we both realize they can do absolutely whatever they want. I can see she's feeling almost as depressed as I am. I mean, without the fear thrown in. Getting on our bikes, we cycle slowly to school, not saying a word to each other the whole way.

*

I sit like a lump of rock at my desk all day. I have absolutely no interest in doing anything or listening to anyone. I don't even bother filling in any answers on my Maths test. There are only two things I convince myself half-heartedly to do: steer clear of Alex at all costs and check my phone every couple of minutes to see if *Baba* or *Anne* have tried phoning me. Or even Elif. The screen remains blank except for text messages from Alex. I know I should delete them but I don't. I save them unopened. I'll read them later on, and I hate myself even more for this.

When Alex comes towards me during break, I duck into the toilets until I hear the bell. I make sure I'm the last person to go into the classroom at the start of each lesson so I can avoid him. There's absolutely no way I'm going to talk to Alex ever again. What a hypocrite I am, acting all innocent now when I should've been doing that yesterday, when it still mattered.

It's the end of the day and we're sitting in Geography, and Mr Stein tells us to go sit with our partners and work on our projects. I'm not going anywhere near Alex. My arm shoots up the second he's finished giving his instructions.

'Zeyneb?' he calls.

'Sir, can I go to the secretary's office? I've got a stomach ache.'

'Now? Can't you wait until the lesson's over?'

I grab hold of my stomach and start groaning. 'No, sir, I think something's wrong with me.'

'Fine. Fine. Go, then. And come straight back when you've . . .'

I'm out of that door so fast I don't hear the rest of his sentence. Of course I don't go to the secretary's office. I go to the reception area with the comfy seats and pot plants where they let the parents and other visitors wait. I sit down and wait for the bell to ring. I know no one will question my presence here because they'll assume I'm waiting for my parents. But then Mr Rubens walks past on his way to the staff room. Now if there's one person I wasn't reckoning on to walk past, it's got to be Mr Rubens. My favourite teacher.

'Zeyneb?' he says, his voice instantly concerned.

I flash him a weak smile and hope he'll carry on past. 'I'm waiting for my mum to fetch me. I'm not feeling well.'

But he doesn't walk past. That would be far too simple for *my* life of rapids and waterfalls. No, he sits down in a chair opposite me. 'Yes, I thought something must be wrong. You didn't write down a single answer on your Maths test this morning. That's not like you.'

Tears are stinging my eyes because, on top of everything that's happening to me, I don't want to add disappointing Mr Rubens to the list.

'I'm not feeling well,' I say feebly.

'I can let you have a second go at the test when you're feeling better,' he suggests.

I nod, without much conviction.

'Because I've got big hopes for you, Zeyneb. You know

that, don't you?'

I shrug.

'You've got a good head on those shoulders of yours, and if you carry on working like you do, you'll be able to go far one day.'

I'm interested. 'You mean, university and stuff?' Sitting forward, I take my arm off my stomach before I remember I'm supposed to be sick. Quickly I put it back again.

'Yes, that's what I mean.' He nods.

'But I'm ...'

'You're what?'

I just blurt it out: 'I'm Muslim. I might have to start wearing a headscarf one of these days.'

Mr Rubens' face turns serious. Either he's thinking, *This is really bad news*, or else he's putting on the concerned-teacher face. I can't tell. 'And this is a problem because ...?'

'Because I really *want* to go to university.'

He massages his chin with his thumb and forefinger for a long time. 'Nothing's stopping you from going with a headscarf, or is there something I'm not seeing here?

'I'm worried that ... I mean, won't it ... send out a kind of message about me?'

'I'm not sure if you should be worrying about that right now. It's true, there will always be people who have views on things like that, but you're never going to be able to please everyone. The best thing someone like you can do, someone with the potential to go a long way, is to do the best you can and leave the intolerant people to themselves.'

'But won't they make it harder for me?'

'They might. There will always be people who make things hard for other people. For you it might be a head-scarf, for someone else it might be not having enough money, or not being clever enough. Life is hard, Zeyneb. That's a fact. But it doesn't mean we should hide away from it.'

I don't want to listen to this. Don't want to hear it. Especially not today. My head's full enough. I'm tired of everyone's good advice. Don't want to think about anything any more.

'There's my mum,' I say, looking through the window at the teachers' car park. I stand up and head towards the door.

'You can take the test again tomorrow if you're feeling better,' he calls after me.

'Goodbye, sir. Thank you,' I say.

I walk out the door and into the car park. Hoping like mad he's not watching me any more, I slip behind a wall and sneak off to the bicycle shed.

I've had enough of this day. Bell or no bell, I'm getting out of here.

17

It's the day of the presentation. I would've stayed at home if I could, pretended to be sick, but *Anne* was having none of it.

'Nonsense. I've seen how hard you and the boy have worked on this project, and you're going to school to do your presentation. I'll put a paracetamol in your lunchbox and you can take it later if you still have tummy ache,' she says.

I grumble some more but she stays firm. Eventually I leave the house and go outside to get my bike. The only thing that cheers me up is the fact that it looks like I've got away with the kiss. Although *Babaanne* seems a little distant, it could just be my imagination, indigestion or something that old people get. *Baba* and *Anne* are treating me normally, so that must mean my grandmother didn't see anything. I have so much on my mind – the whole mess with Alex, our presentation, what Mr Rubens said yesterday about wearing a headscarf – I'm relieved not to have to worry about *Babaanne* too.

Relieved – that's an understatement.

Geography is second period and Mr Stein is making quite a big deal out of this presentation. It's obviously going to count for a stack of marks and I'm glad Alex and I worked so hard on it. We're sitting in the IT classroom and Mr Stein's setting up the projector. He's invited the other Geography teacher and her form class to sit in on our presentation. Next week we'll get the chance to see theirs.

There's quite a buzz in the classroom as partners huddle together, going over the last details of their projects. Some of them have these huge posters with images of weather stuck on them. Alex and I only have a PowerPoint so luckily there's nothing we have to discuss.

Or, at least, that's what I think. But Alex has got this huge box covered with a Barcelona football flag, and he carries it towards me with an enormous grin. What on earth does he have in there? A cake? A puppy? A human head? I have no idea.

The only thing I do know is that I don't want to speak to him.

Jumping up from my seat, I rush to the front of the class. 'Can I help you with something, sir?' I say, almost bumping into Mr Stein.

'Thanks, but I've got it all under control, Zeyneb,' he says. 'Go back to your seat. We're going to start in a few minutes.'

I have no choice but to return to Alex, standing there

with his box, his dimple, his black fringe over one eye and an expectant look on his face. No choice but to return to the knowledge of what we did four days ago. Everyone else is busy and I can hardly go stand next to some other couple and start helping them with *their* project.

'Zeyneb?' He's still smiling, but he's chewing his bottom lip too. I want to say sorry. After all, it's not *his* fault that I'm not allowed to kiss a boy.

'You want to see what I made?' He puts the box down on an empty desk and pulls off the football flag. I stare inside.

There's this big papier-mâché thing lying at the bottom of the box. I can see he used a balloon for a frame. It's got these tinfoil-covered protrusions and small mirrors on the surface.

'It's a weather satellite,' he says, even though I see right away what it is. Haven't we just spent the last ten days looking up everything about it? 'My dad and I spent two days building it. I thought maybe we could get some extra marks for it.'

I must admit, it's really good. But a part of me is still cross with him – well, not cross exactly, but . . . I'm not ready to go back to talking to him as if nothing's happened.

'Since when did we agree on building a model for the project?' I ask, and I can hear how I sound: demanding, unreasonable.

It's his turn to sound cross. 'I've been trying to get hold

of you, Zeyneb, trying to talk to you about it, but you won't answer your phone, won't reply to my texts. What was I supposed to do?'

I'm about to say something when Mr Stein interrupts us. 'All right, everyone, quiet now. Take your seats, please.'

Alex and I quickly sit down. Kelly and David are called up to the front first. They give a presentation about how mankind has developed the ability to change certain weather patterns. It's not bad. As Kelly passes my chair to go back to her seat I give her a thumbs-up. Next up are Celeste and Mustafa, and they're talking about extreme weather. After them we listen to Jamal and Nicole, Christine and Matt, and then, at last, Mr Stein calls Alex and me to the front.

We've practised really hard for this. I look at Alex and see him wiping his palms on his trousers. I realize my palms are sweaty as well. We ask Mr Stein to turn off the lights and then we start the PowerPoint and go through the different slides of weather satellites, how they work, the images they send down to earth . . .

I do the explanation for one slide and Alex for the next, just like we practised. Everything's going smoothly. I don't notice anyone fiddling or whispering or anything. Celeste's resting her chin on her hand, Jamal's mouth is open, gaping, as if we're explaining some dead complicated move in football or something. I bite my bottom lip to hold back a smile. They're liking it. No one looks bored. This feels great! Every couple of seconds I see

Mr Stein giving a little nod in our direction. I know we're doing well. I love this feeling when I see all my efforts have paid off.

We get to the last slide and then it's up to Alex to unveil his model. Mr Stein turns the lights back on and gives permission for everyone to come to the front to take a closer look at Alex's weather satellite. The two of us step back to let our classmates crowd around the table.

I can see by the twitching of Alex's mouth that he wants to break out into a grin too but that he's keeping it in, like me. My lips are pressed together so I don't look like a grinning, goofy idiot.

'I think they liked it,' Alex whispers.

I nod. 'I know. I'm sorry, it's a good weather satellite.'

'You can have it if you like.'

I smile. 'No, I couldn't. You must've spent ages working on it.'

'I did, but I made it for you. To say sorry. For kiss— for getting you into trouble.'

Don't be sorry, I want to say. 'I didn't get into trouble,' I say instead.

He gives a big sigh. 'Good. I'm glad.'

'I love my satellite,' I add. And not just any old satellite: an Alex-handmade-weather-satellite.

'OK, thank you, everybody. You can sit back down now.' It's Mr Stein again. He's come up behind Alex and me and he rests a hand lightly on our shoulders. 'Well done, you two. That was very good.'

We fall in with the throng and return to our seats. I've

got the box clutched tightly to my chest. Mr Stein calls the next pair to the front for their presentation.

'Does that mean you'll come to the funfair this weekend?' Alex whispers.

I look down at my beautiful weather satellite and all my doubts, all my decisions to do the right thing, fly out of the window to join the real satellites out there in space.

I nod.

18

I keep telling myself I'm doing nothing wrong. Alex has apologized for kissing me, even gave me a weather satellite to say sorry. Going to the funfair with a bunch of kids from my class – what can be more innocent than that? I repeat it over and over to myself. Loudly. So I drown out the other voice that's there, or at least try to. The other voice that's saying: *You're doing it again, Zeyneb. Going behind their backs. Liking this boy too much.*

I'm standing by the Big Swing with Kelly. It's five o'clock, the time we've arranged to meet the others. My father dropped us off and gave me the usual lecture about what to do and what not. I didn't hear a word he said. The others are coming by bus: Julie, Christine, Jamal, David, Matt and Alex.

'Do I look OK?' I ask Kelly, adjusting my top for about the tenth time so it hangs properly and doesn't draw too much attention to my flat chest. She laughs.

'What?' I demand.

'You know, you've never asked me that before.'

'So what?' I snap. 'I want to look nice. What's wrong with that?'

'Nothing.' She smiles. 'And you do look nice. Practically the same as every other day I see you, but still, nice.'

'And my shoes?' I ask.

'They look the same as your other trainers,' she says.

'They are,' I say dejectedly. 'I bought them at the same shop.'

She grins at me. 'Face it, Zey, they're never going to make Barbie dolls out of either of us.'

I nod, but at the same time I'm thinking how I should've stopped off at Elif's house and maybe put on a touch of eyeliner. That new blue one I saw her wearing last week.

Someone's warm hands come from behind and cover my eyes. Simply from the way my skin tingles, I know whose hands they are. Laughing, I duck to escape and turn to face him. Of course, it's Alex. Behind him are his friends, all hair gel and grins at the prospect of spending an evening at the funfair with a bunch of girls, even if the girls are the same ones they see every day in class.

Next to Jamal is a girl about a head shorter than him. She looks nervous and feisty at the same time. I'm sure I've seen her somewhere before.

'My sister, Leyla.' He shrugs. 'My parents made me bring her along.'

My heart almost stands still when I see another girl emerge from behind Leyla. It's Semra, my cousin!

'What are you doing here?' I demand.

'*Anne* said I could come with Leyla,' says Semra. 'We're in the same class at school. Anyway, your mum told mine you'd be here and you could keep an eye on us.'

I can't believe my mum has just let my cousin tag along without even asking me! This is so typical! I remember when I was a little girl how I'd just be palmed off on to older cousins and how they hated it. And now the wheel has turned and I'm standing here with sticking-her-nose-into-everything-Semra. Tonight, of all nights!

'Can't you just get your own life?' I glare at her. She sticks out her tongue at me.

Leyla says to her brother, 'You'd better be nice to us, or I'll tell Mum.'

He promptly turns round and pushes her. Not hard, but hard enough for her to almost lose her balance. 'How about not being such a squirt?' he says.

Walking really quickly to leave the two girls behind, we go to stand in the queue for the Big Swing. Alex offers to pay for me, but that suddenly makes me feel like I'm on a date.

'You said only friends,' I remind him, and he shrugs and shoves the money back in his pocket.

We're having a great time. We've been on Velocity Force, the Terminator and the bumper cars. And even though Jamal and David and Matt are usually such dorks, we're all laughing and teasing one another. Whenever Leyla and Semra appear at our side, we fob them off with some errand or other: *Buy us a Coke, buy us another Coke,*

140

you're too young for this ride, how about that one there – it looks like fun . . .

We're queuing to get tickets for the Dive Bomber. My money's almost finished and I still want to go on the Breakdancer but I don't want to say anything. Everyone else seems to have an endless amount of cash.

I step out of the queue. 'Hey, I'm going to sit this one out. I want some candyfloss,' I say.

'But it's almost our turn,' David states the obvious.

'I know, but I really don't feel like going on this one. I'll be back before you guys are off.'

I set off in search of the candyfloss van. Behind me I hear the sound of feet crunching in the gravel.

'You OK?' It's Alex. He slows down to walk next to me.

'I'm fine. I'll be back in five minutes,' I say.

'I want to get a drink,' he says. 'Besides, my parents aren't exactly millionaires. My money's almost finished.'

'Mine too.' I smile.

He moves a little closer to me and we walk on, side by side. It feels good to have him next to me like this. But the voice from earlier is back and it slams into my head: *You're doing it again, Zeyneb! You're liking him too much.*

Trying to be subtle, I move away from him.

'I'm not going to bite you,' he says.

I come to a stop and step into the space between two stalls. I'm going to tell him. I'm going to make it clear. I don't know where this decision has come from all of a sudden, but it's here and I'm fine with it. My parents think I'm on the Big Swing with Kelly while I'm actually walking with a boy I like more than is good for me. A boy who kissed me. I don't want to do this to them. Taking a very deep breath, I start:

'I . . . I think you know that I like you, Alex?'

'I like you too,' he says, his eyes all serious and understanding. If he carries on looking at me like that, I won't be able to say what I need to say, so I turn my head away and stare at the writing on the side of the stall claiming to have the best chips in the country.

'You know it's different with us . . . with us Muslim kids. I've told you this before. We're not allowed to have boyfriends or girlfriends at this age. It's strictly forbidden.'

'But I know other Turkish girls who have boyfriends,' he says.

'I know. There are some who do, but I don't want to be one of them. Those girls are always scared of getting found out and, most of the time, it comes out anyway. I know because my sister was one of them. Look, my parents are who they are. I don't want to go behind their backs like this.'

His fringe flops over his eyes and he looks sad. 'But I thought we agreed to be friends?'

'We tried that and it didn't really work, did it? It isn't even working now.'

He takes a step closer to me and his hands reach automatically for mine. His long fingers curl gently around my own, warming my hands inside his. I want to pull back but he looks so sad I don't have the heart to do it.

'But I really like you, Zeyneb. I don't want to go back to how it was before, just classmates.'

'You'll find other girls to like,' I say, but I hate the way that sounds.

'And you, will you find other boys to like?'

'I hope not. This is much too complicated for me. I just want to finish school and go to university and then figure things out from there.'

His grip on my fingers tightens. 'I don't want to let you go.'

My insides absolutely melt. I don't want to do this. I don't want to have this conversation. I'm longing to tell him, 'Then don't,' and fall into his arms and have those soft lips kiss me again. I want . . .

But I'm going to stick to my decision.

'Being a good Muslim is who I am, Alex. I can't change that. I don't *want* to change it.'

'But you're not like the others. You're tough and you stand up for yourself and you're clever. You don't run around with that whole headscarf crowd . . .'

My heart starts to sink. 'Headscarf crowd?'

'That clique at school. You know, the ones who all wear headscarves and act as if they're holier than the rest of us.'

Now I see panic in his eyes. He realizes he's said the wrong thing and he doesn't know how to unsay it.

'And what if I start wearing a headscarf? Will you still like me then?'

'But you won't. That's just the point. You're Zeyneb.

You're . . . you're . . .'

'I've been thinking about it,' I say, jutting out my chin.

'Serious?'

I nod and carry on staring into those eyes.

It's him who looks away this time. 'But why?' he asks.

'Because that's who I am. That's what I've been trying to tell you.'

Neither of us has to say anything more. A line has been drawn between us and neither of us can cross to the other side ever again. I can't be with a boy who thinks that way about me, about us. Even if everything else weren't standing in our way, it would never work.

I'm about to untangle my hands from his when I hear a shrill voice pipe up next to us: 'I thought you were going to get candyfloss?'

It's Leyla – somehow she's managed to track us down. Quickly we let go of each other's hands. Did she see us? My heart is banging against my chest but I try to sound as casual as possible: 'We're on our way.'

I step out from between the stalls. Alex joins me, but further away than before. My banging heart quietens down. I'm sad, but then again I'm not. I can't really explain it. I feel like . . . I feel like . . . I'm OK.

'Move it, Leyla,' Alex snaps at her. 'Why can't you stay with your brother? Since when did we become your babysitters?'

She trots up to us and squeezes herself in the middle.

There are goosebumps on the back of my neck but I try to play it innocent: 'Where's Semra?'

144

'She's queuing for the toilets,' Leyla says.

'You left her alone?' I ask.

'I'm going back now.'

I glance down at her. Alex looks at her too. We both spot it at the same time. It's hard to describe exactly, but we know what we've seen. A glint. One minute she's this irritating little girl, the next she's got this look of pure calculating evil in her eye. A shiver runs through my whole body.

'You say anything to Zeyneb's cousin and I'll tell Jamal I caught you smoking,' Alex says.

'But that's not true . . .' she whines.

'Don't care. I'll tell him anyway. Now move.'

I bite my lip and don't say anything.

At last we come to a stop in front of the candyfloss stall. Alex asks for a Coke. I don't feel like anything any more. I just want to go home.

Leyla steps to the front. 'That big bag over there,' she says loudly, 'will you buy it for me?'

19

It's ten past nine and I'm supposed to have been picked up by my father in the car park behind the funfair ten minutes ago. They don't like me catching the bus home when it gets dark. But he hasn't arrived yet and I'm wondering what's happened. *Baba* is never late. I try phoning him but he doesn't answer.

Kelly's mum pulls up to fetch her. 'You want a ride home?' she asks.

'I'd better not. My father's probably on his way, and if he gets here and I'm not . . .'

'Then we'll wait with you. Jump in the car. It's cold outside.'

The three of us sit shivering in the car. Annelies leaves the engine running to keep the heating on, but it's still cold. My eyes follow each set of headlights that approaches, only to be disappointed when it turns out not to be *Baba*.

'You sure he said nine o'clock?' Annelies asks.

'I'm sure.'

I try his phone again. Nothing. I try my mum's. I phone the house. Nothing. I'm starting to think something's wrong. Kelly and her mum sense it too.

Eventually it's half past. Annelies stubs out her cigarette in the ashtray and says, 'I'm taking you home, Zeyneb. Surely your dad will phone you when he gets here and doesn't find you.'

I don't know what to say. I know they want to go home, but I also know I can't agree to go with them. Just then I see a set of headlights drawing up slowly. I squint to make out the model of the car. It's Elif's. Now I know for certain that something's not right.

'My sister's here,' I say feebly.

'What's wrong?' Kelly asks, turning round in her seat to look at me.

'I've got to go.'

I slam the car door and wait for Elif to draw up next to me. The car stops. I drop into the passenger seat and turn towards my sister. Only it's not her in the driver's seat. It's Deniz.

'Where's Elif?' I gasp.

'She's at your house.'

'What's happened?'

But he doesn't answer. He just shakes his head and puts the car into first gear. At least no one's died, I think, or else he wouldn't be behaving like this. I'm chewing my nails, watching the city lights outside, trying to guess what's wrong. Surely it's got nothing to do with me? Surely they couldn't have found out about . . .

At last we pull up outside our house. *Baba*'s car is in the driveway. So is *Teyze*'s, Semra's mum.

Now I know. One bag of candyfloss wasn't enough to keep Leyla quiet – she told Semra about me and Alex. I just can't believe how quickly it's come home.

I let myself out of the car without looking at Deniz.

With feet that feel like they've got rocks tied to them, I walk up the steps to our front door. Bending down, I slip off the new shoes I'd been so proud of just a few hours earlier and put on my slippers. Taking hold of the door handle, I turn it.

My whole family's sitting there, same as the last time. Only this is worse. Much, much worse.

I can see *Anne*'s been crying, so has Elif. *Baba*'s looking down at the carpet, his head in his hands. I've never seen him sit like this before. No one looks at me when I come in. No one says a word. Not to me. Not to one another. Then I see Semra's there too, and she's got her face buried in her mother's side. How I hope she'll have many, many secret boyfriends in years to come. How I hope she wears short skirts and revealing tops. I'm going to make it my personal ambition to hunt her down and bust her to her spiteful mother every single time. Why do they get so much pleasure from bringing bad news into my family? Why are they out to destroy my life? What have I ever done to them?

'Hello, *Baba*. Hello, *Anne*. Hello, *Teyze*. Elif, Semra,' I say politely, like a robot. It's either that or I break down in front of everyone. Of course, no one acknowledges me. Well, Elif sneaks me a look to let me know she's on my side, but she doesn't dare greet me. This must bring back so many memories for her, except for the fact that she was older when she met Deniz, which makes me look even worse.

The atmosphere is so thick I can hardly breathe. I just stand there. I know I'm expected to go to my room and think about the shame I've brought on my family, but I can't get myself to cross the floor. It's as if the air's going to run out before I reach the stairs and I'll suffocate. I notice *Babaanne*'s not sitting here with the others. I wonder briefly where she is.

'What are you just standing there for? Get to your room. Get out of my sight,' *Baba* barks, raising his head from his hands. 'I'll deal with you later.'

He's never spoken to me like that before. Never once told me to get out of his sight. My legs come back to life and I hurry through the lounge and up the stairs. Opening and closing my bedroom door for the benefit of everyone downstairs, I tiptoe down the passage to my grandmother's room.

'*Babaanne*?' I whisper at the door.

I hear rustling inside.

'*Babaanne*?'

The door opens and she's standing in front of me in her long white nightdress. Her grey hair, released from its daytime bun, falls softly on her shoulders. I want to fall into her arms. I want her to hold me.

'You must go to your bedroom now, *kizim*.'

'But—'

'No, Zeyneb, I cannot give you refuge in my bedroom while your parents are sitting downstairs feeling betrayed. It wouldn't be right.'

'But I didn't do anything,' I whisper.

Her face becomes stern, her voice harsh. 'Don't make it worse by lying. Own up to what you've done and find a way to make it right again.'

'But *Babaanne*—'

'I saw you, Zeyneb. I saw you in the garden with that boy. It's insulting to stand here and be lied to by someone as young as you.'

My mouth is hanging wide open. 'You didn't say anything?'

'No, I didn't, and now I think I made the wrong decision. I thought to myself: *Zeyneb is a sensible girl. She'll do the right thing.* But I misjudged you. I don't know. Maybe you're still too young for any sense to have taken hold in there?'

Suddenly we hear the stairs groan under my father's footsteps. He doesn't come all the way up but stops halfway and calls out to his mother, '*Anne*, let the child go to her room, please. She is punished.'

'She's going, son,' she calls back.

I try to meet her eyes but she looks away from me. Stepping back, she closes her bedroom door in my face. I hear my father walk slowly down the stairs again. I go to my room.

She misjudged me. That's what she said. *Babaanne.* I'm too young for any sense to have taken hold in my head. How could she say that? How could those words come out of *my Babaanne*'s mouth?

Sense! I have plenty of sense. Haven't I just done the most difficult thing in my entire life by sending Alex away *because* I have sense? Haven't I spent the past weeks struggling over my decision to wear a headscarf, weighing up the pros and cons, speaking to just about everybody I could find, *because* I have sense?

I'm the most sensible girl I know and yet they're all looking at me like I don't exist! Is it sensible for my eleven-year-old cousin to run off and bust me before I've even had a chance to get home? Is it sensible for *Teyze*, a grown-up, to be so pleased when she sees one of us fall? Is it sensible for my parents to jump to conclusions before they've heard my side of the story? To be so worried about what the outside world thinks that they can't even stop to listen to their daughter, their own flesh and blood?

How is it possible that *I'm* the one being accused of having no sense?

Now I'm furious. I phone Kelly and, in an angry whisper, spew out everything that's happened.

'Oh, Zeyneb,' she says quietly. 'Do you want me to ask my mum to bring me over to your place? I can tell them you didn't do anything with Alex the whole night.'

'They're not interested in the truth, Kel, or else they would've asked for my side of the story too.'

'What are they going to do to you?'

'I don't know. They might keep me home till the summer holidays and then cart me off to *Babaanne*'s in Turkey. Or they'll send me to another school, like I said.' I sigh. 'I don't know. But they'll find a way to make sure I can't look at another boy for the rest of my life.'

'Do you mean that?'

'I don't know what they're going to do, Kel, but one thing I'm sure about is that I'm not going to get off lightly.'

'I'll speak to my mum,' she offers.

'What can she do?'

'I don't know. I just want to help.'

'It's OK. I'll be fine. I'm not going to sit around this house with a bunch of hypocrites and wait for *them* to decide my fate.'

Actually the words just pour out of my mouth before I've had a chance to think about them, but now that they're out, they feel powerful. Yes, that's what I'm going to do. I'm going to leave this stupid house, leave all these people who think I'm so *senseless* and go somewhere else. Somewhere I'll be accepted for who I am. Somewhere I'll actually be listened to for once.

'If they phone, just tell them you haven't heard from me, all right? And don't say anything to your mum.'

'Are you serious?'

'I am.'

'Zeyneb, don't do anything stupid.'

'I'll be fine, Kel. I promise.'

'You can come stay with us.'

'That's the first place they'll look.'

'I'll hide you in my room. I won't say anything to my mum.'

'I can't ask you to lie to her.'

'I don't mind. It's for a good reason.'

'I've got to go, Kel.'

'Promise me you'll phone me tomorrow?' she says.

'I will,' I say, but I don't promise.

I'm sitting on my bed, staring at the phone in my hands. *Not sensible!* Not sensible!

That's when it comes to me. Like a flash. Suddenly I know exactly what I'm going to do.

I get up on the edge of my bed and reach for my small travel bag on top of my cupboard. I grab a bunch of clothes from the shelf and throw them in, then stuff all my pocket money into my jeans pocket.

Why must they treat me this way? Like I've done something so terrible. Like I've disgraced them. Like I'm not their daughter.

Without meaning to, I burst into tears. And even though I don't know why I'm crying, it makes me feel even more angry.

I'll show them what sensible is. *I'll show them!*

20

Carefully I drop my bag from my bedroom window and hear it thud on to the ground. Then I sit on the windowsill and, clutching the ivy growing up the wall, I swing my legs out and try to find a foothold on the wooden trellis. Carefully I inch down, but the trellis ends halfway down. I'm going to have to jump the last bit.

I land with another thud next to my travel bag, and hear the ice on the grass crackle beneath my feet. It's cold tonight, unusually cold for this time of the year. Not good news for the cherry blossoms in our garden, I think, then put that out of my mind.

I keep quiet, listening carefully. Has anyone heard me? But the outside light doesn't go on and the murmur of voices from the lounge stays the same. Still talking about me. I'm safe.

Reaching for my bag, I get up and tiptoe as quietly as I can to the back gate. The air I breathe out is white with condensation and my fingers are freezing. I bunch my free hand up inside my sleeve. Should've brought my gloves. And worn a warmer jacket. I'll be OK, I tell myself bravely. I'm not going to fold at the first sign of a bit of cold.

I try to open the back gate. Quietly. We hardly ever use it, so it's jammed shut. Plus my fingers are so cold and stiff they're not working properly. The neighbours' stupid dog starts barking and I almost jump out of my skin. At last I get the dumb gate open and I set off down the back alley.

Let them sit there, gathered together so cosily, ganging up on me. I don't care. I'd like to see them in the morning when I don't show up for breakfast. What are they going to do then? I'll be long gone and they'll wish . . . they'll wish . . . they'll wish they had treated me properly. I shove my hand into the back pocket of my jeans to feel the notebook tucked away there: *Anne*'s little black notebook with *Teyze* Havva's address on it. My mystery aunt. I know there's a bus that goes directly there – I checked the timetable. She won't turn me away, will she? I'll go to school there and be friends with whoever I want. I'll show them who has no sense.

But it's a long way to the bus station. I hope no one sees me.

I walk down to the end of my street and turn left. Two of the street lights are out, but I don't let the dark get to me. I carry on, left again at the dilapidated bench, and right two roads down. I get to the street with the shops: a pet shop, a small supermarket, a bankrupt pizza place. All the lights are off. I decide to go down the alley at the back, just in case someone we know happens to drive along and see me.

I make my way down the alley. It's only as I get to the end, where it opens out on to another, quieter street, that I see the orange glow of a fire crackling inside some kind of metal drum. And around it are figures, probably tramps, warming their hands, talking, laughing. I stop, hovering uncertainly. Will they notice me? I don't think I dare walk past. But I don't want to go back to the main road either.

I conjure up a picture of the street on the other side of the alley. I could quickly climb over a garden wall and get through one of the gardens. I try to remember which of these houses has a dog and pick one. *Please, Allah, let me be right, let the owners not have a dog!*

I'm surprised by how high the wall is. Much higher than I thought. Putting down my bag, I go back a few steps and then take a little run-up. I try to get hold of the top of the wall but I scrape the skin off my fingers. Luckily it's so cold I hardly feel a thing.

I try again. And again. My fingers are scraped raw and my knees bash against the wall. This isn't going to work. I'm going to go back out on to the main street. Surely no one will be out at this time of the night.

But as I turn round, I notice one of the figures has left the fire and is coming towards me. A dark figure, hunched up, white breath coming out of his face. He's closing the space between us rapidly – there's suddenly no time for me to run to the end of the alley.

'Hey,' he shouts at me. 'Hey, you!'

Now I really *have* to get over this wall. My breathing is fast and shallow.

Turning round, I spot something big and dark – a dustbin. Why didn't I see that before? As quickly as I can, I scramble on top of it.

The man is still coming towards me, breaking into a run. I hear him breathing hoarsely, in and out, his foot-steps crunching on the gravel. *Baba* always told me that if someone looked threatening it meant they probably were.

I pull myself up on to the wall and crouch there. Before I look back. My bag! It's lying on the ground next to the dustbin.

'Stop!' I hear his voice behind me.

Never mind about the bag. Taking a deep breath, I jump.

The moment I hit the ground I hear a loud crack. It seems to have come from my shin. A pain like I've never felt before sears through my leg.

I'm lying on jagged bits of rock or something, my knee pulled up to my chest, and I'm rocking, groaning, crying with pain. My eyes are stinging and I want to scream but I don't want the owners of the house to find me, to phone the police, or – worse – my parents.

I have no idea how long I've been lying here, but I can't hear the man shouting any more. And I'm numb all over from the cold. Could have been five minutes, or an hour.

I can't feel anything, not even the leg that cracked. Cautiously I sit up and look around. I've landed on a pile of rubble and wood. No wonder I fell so badly: I just didn't see it in the dark. My leg throbs as I pull myself up, and I groan – can't help it. Yes, that definitely still hurts.

The back light from the house next door goes on. I stand dead still, all my weight on my good leg. Is it a motion sensor? Did somebody hear me? I wait, but I see nothing. I'm going to have to keep my big mouth shut. Where am I? If it was daytime, I'd be able to figure it out, but right now the cold is making my brain woozy.

Feeling around, I find a stick that looks about the right size and, putting it under my armpit like a crutch, I hop forward. My leg jolts and I want to scream, but bite my lip instead. I taste blood.

I've gone past the mosque and now I'm slinking along behind the trees so I don't get spotted. Above my head I hear the wind rushing furiously through the leaves. I pull the sleeves of my flimsy jumper over my fingers. In the distance a dog barks. Each step takes forever – at least, that's how it feels. It's taken me absolutely ages to get this far. I check my mobile – almost one o'clock. At least another four hours before the sun comes up. I need to be at the bus station by then, otherwise some do-gooder driver is going to find me and drag me off to hospital or something. My leg's fine, I tell myself – just a sprain.

Just keep on moving, Zeyneb. Keep on moving.

At last – at long, long last – I see the bus station. And

next to it *Baba*'s allotment. I was going to get to the bus station and hop straight on a bus – but the first bus isn't until morning. I really need to get out of the cold for a while, away from anyone who might be at the station.

By the light of a street lamp, I see his red cabbage seedlings standing neatly in a row. I can just imagine *Anne* boiling cabbage leaves a few months from now before she stuffs them with mince. My stomach lets out a groan just at the thought of it and tears spring to my eyes. And now everything starts hurting again. My shin, my frozen fingers, my knees, the skin under my armpit from my makeshift crutch . . . As I think of the warmth inside the shed, the familiar smell of the mouldy hessian sacks piled in the corner, the tears – of relief now – trickle over my cheeks.

I expect to see the sun coming up any minute. Taking out my phone, I check the time: 2:56 a.m. and 1°C. That's cold for spring. And still a couple of hours of darkness left. I'm exhausted. I just need to sleep. I have no idea what I'm going to do to keep myself warm. Why didn't I think of bringing a sleeping bag? *Never mind, I'll be fine.*

I open the rusty, creaking gate to the allotment and I'm met by all the usual smells –the clay soil, pungent rosemary, the pile of decomposing leaves . . . I know *Baba*'s trays of courgette and pumpkin seedlings are to the left of me inside his little greenhouse. I see the young fennel shoots just peeping out of the ground and wonder if they'll survive this cold snap. Before I go into the shed, I stuff some lettuce leaves into my mouth but they do nothing to relieve my hunger.

Lifting the latch to let myself in, I drop down into a corner. At least I'm out of the wind. I pull two hessian sacks over my body, put my head down on a bag of compost and close my eyes. Why didn't I buy that candyfloss at the funfair last night? I might've been less hungry. As I'm tumbling into sleep, images swim before me: *Baba*'s face, a row of aubergines, Alex, red cabbages, Zehra . . .

But no! Something jolts inside me and my eyes fly open. I'm remembering that documentary about the family who got lost in a forest in Germany or Austria or somewhere and how half of them froze to death. If I allow myself to fall asleep then I might not wake up in the morning. *Am I being ridiculous?* I have no idea. But however angry I am with with *Baba*, with *Babaanne* and *Anne*, however sweet the revenge would be if I died because of them, that they'd be sorry for the rest of their lives, I don't actually *want* to die. I have to stay awake.

Taking my phone out of my pocket again, I scroll down to *K* and push Kelly's number. I suddenly really need to talk to my friend, to hear her to tell me it's going to be OK. But it goes over to voicemail. And I feel more alone than ever.

Soon I'm freezing. My teeth are chattering like a monkey's. I've got the hessian sacks wrapped all the way around me, but I might as well be sitting here naked for all the good they're doing. I want to cry, but it just seems like so much effort right now. Every cell in my body is fighting to stay awake.

I have no idea what I'm going to do. My eyes are heavy and I'm fighting to keep them open. And what about my leg? I edge it out of the hessian sacks and look down. I gasp.

My leg has swollen up to elephant proportions. The flesh is straining at the seams of my jeans, and the bit of exposed skin between my sock and my trouser leg is shiny. And it's purple. I've never seen anything like it before. My heart sinks – it's more than a sprain. I know that much. But I can't, just *can't*, ring the hospital.

I lean forward to take a closer look at it and suddenly my leg lets me know it's still there: the worst ever pain shoots from my toes to my hip. I can't help the scream that comes out. It feels like I'm going to shoot through the roof. Closing my eyes, I breathe in deeply. I'm suddenly dizzy, like I'm going to faint.

Why did my stupid leg have to go and spoil my plans! Stupid leg! Stupid wall that I jumped over! Stupid figure by the fire that came after me.

I don't want to be left here, all alone, in the dark, in the cold, unable to walk. But for now, I don't see any other option. I just need some time to think. Time to figure things out. To think of the next step.

21

Even though I'm trying not to, I fall asleep. Then wake up. Fall asleep again. Wake up. Where on earth am I?

Baba's shed – it suddenly comes flooding back to me. I'm inside the shed. My leg! I groan. It's absolutely killing me. It's throbbing like there's some little elf inside it, hammering away on the bone. I'm not sure . . . is it possible? . . . it feels even worse than before . . .

There's a small window in one of the walls in *Baba*'s shed and I notice it's starting to become just a bit lighter outside. I can't wait for dawn. The dark and the cold together are unbearable. Even though I've got the hessian bags wrapped around me, the cold still manages to creep in underneath and touch me everywhere: my hands, my toes, my nose, my back, my arms . . .

I stare out through the window at the dark grey sky, attempting to focus. Birds fly overhead. I try to identify them, call their names out loud: 'Crow . . . magpie . . . swallow . . .'

I'll give my leg a couple more hours to rest, I decide,

and then I'll make my way to the bus station. It's probably about a minute's walk from here under normal circumstances. With my leg like this, I estimate it will take me fifteen minutes, but it will be worth it. I'll get on a bus and go speeding off to *Teyze* Havva and I'll never look back. She'll take care of my leg when I get there, like *Anne* would. I wonder if she has a garden, whether she makes *sarmas* . . .

Tears sting my eyes but I don't let them out. I force myself to think about something else . . . like, will someone recognise me on the bus? Then I see *Baba*'s cap that he wears when he's gardening, hanging on a peg behind the door. I'm about to drag myself up to get it when I hear it.

The creaking of the allotment gate.

Then footsteps. Heavy footsteps. A man's. But not *Baba*'s. I'd pick out the sound of his footsteps anywhere. No, these belong to a stranger. For a moment I'm back in the alley, the figure racing towards me.

Hide, Zeyneb, hide! I tell myself. I'm short of breath. Where? Where?

The footsteps are getting closer.

I look around the shed: at the airtight plastic containers where my dad keeps his seeds; the plastic table and two chairs that he puts outside in the summertime; the orange hosepipe on a reel; bags of compost piled on top of one another; an old, waist-high kitchen cabinet that my dad dragged in here to keep his odds and ends.

That's it. I'll squeeze in there.

Throwing the hessian sacks off my body, I start dragging myself across the floor with my hands, pushing with my good leg. Pain shoots through my body, but I've got no time to think about that now.

In between the sound of my body swishing over the floor, in the little flashes of silence, I can hear that the footsteps have reached the shed. But, instead of coming inside, whoever it is is walking around outside. Slowly. As if he's got all the time in the world.

I'm at the cupboard and I'm yanking at the little handle, but it won't open. I pull and pull. Then I remember: the key! *Baba* keeps the cupboard locked. Other gardeners have had stuff taken from their sheds. He hides the key under an upturned flowerpot by the seedling trays. I lunge towards it, knock it over and grab the key. Shoving it into the keyhole, I turn. I hear the click of the mechanism as it unlocks.

The footsteps have gone all the way around the shed. I'm expecting the door to open any moment now. I'm crawling into the cupboard on one knee, pushing things out on to the floor as quickly and quietly as I can to make room: cartons of apple juice, a bag of biscuits, a wooden box . . . I crouch down, squash into the corner and turn round so I can get hold of my broken leg. It's throbbing, burning, currents of pain shooting right up to my hip, but I don't have time to be careful with it. Biting down hard on my lip to stifle a scream, I put both hands around my knee and yank hard, pulling my leg into the cupboard after me. I grab at the door with my raw fingers to close it, glancing quickly up at the window.

A man's standing there. He's looking in, cupping his face with two hands. It's still too dark to make out his features. Who could be creeping around the allotment at this time of the morning? I pull the door shut and try to catch my breath. Darkness. *Calm down, Zeyneb. Breathe.* Footsteps again. They stop at the shed door and it opens. No! It's not possible. *This is not possible!* The footsteps come inside and a glimmer of light shines into the cupboard through the keyhole. I smell cigarettes, and soil mixed with sweat. I hear him cross the floor, the sound of rustling, then something hard knocks against wood. Shoving my eye up against the keyhole, I try to see what's going on.

I can't see the whole of him. Just his arm. It's up against the back wall, touching my dad's gardening tools one by one.

Dark-green jacket, a checked shirt pocket underneath, I can't see more. He's moving again to the opposite corner. The corner I've just escaped from, with the pile of hessian sacks. I re-adjust my head inside the tiny cupboard to follow his movements. He's bending down. I can see a pair of muddy jeans. He's scratching around on the floor. Then he straightens up and I see he's got *Baba's* secateurs in his hand. What's he going to do with them?

Just as a scream is building in my throat, I see the back of his left foot – he's wearing a pair of old trainers, covered in mud, his heel squashing down the back of his shoe.

Ali! It's Ali. I'd recognize those shoes of his anywhere. The guy who has the allotment next to my father's. They're always swapping seedlings with each other. He's the one who gave *Baba* those yellow chilli plants he was so chuffed about. But *Baba* was just telling me last week how the new hose nozzle he'd bought had disappeared. Now I can tell him what happened to it. That Ali probably 'borrowed' it.

But I can't, I remember suddenly. I can't tell *Baba* anything ever again.

I hear the latch of the shed lift and the door bang. Then footsteps, and the creaking of the gate. He's gone. Ali's gone.

Silence.

Pain.

I collapse against the cupboard door. It gives way and my body spills out on to the floor. I don't care. I lie there.

My head is pounding. My leg is pounding. My heart is pounding. And hot. Suddenly I'm so very, very hot. My body is covered in sweat.

If only I hadn't jumped over that wall last night. I should be sitting on a bus, zooming away from my parents, from Alex, from school, for ever. From Kelly too, I realize with a stab in my chest. I'll probably never see her again either when I start my new life . . .

I'm crying. Stupid, I know. I've cried more tonight than in the whole of my life. Warm tears run down my cheeks and I don't bother to wipe them away. They're tears of pain, real physical pain like I've never felt in all my life, but also tears for my old life. Maybe Kelly will be secretly glad that I'm not going to be around any more – complicated Zeyneb with all her weird problems. How soon will she find a new best friend? And all my other friends. Mr Rubens . . . Boring Mr Stein. I'll never see my parents again either, even though I hate them right now, even though I can never forgive them for being so wrong, so unfair . . . My tears turn to loud sobs, my shoulders shaking.

Why am I so hot when I've been so cold until now? And so thirsty. . . I want to get up, to get going, but I can't seem to move from the cupboard. It's . . . too much . . . Too much effort. I'll just rest for a while . . .

My leg's hurting. My whole body's hurting. My skin is on fire and my mouth is so dry. I try to lean out of the cupboard to grab what might be a bottle of water, but *Baba*'s suddenly in front of me and he kicks it out of reach. He hovers over me, his face contorted like a monster, and he's yelling, 'Get out of my sight!'

Behind him I see Alex. He's nodding at Baba, urging him on, laughing at me . . . 'I had fun being with you,' he says, 'but not any more.'

I want to call out to him. Ask him to stop. Ask him for water – ask him . . .

And there's *Babaanne* . . . 'I misjudged you,' she's saying as she plaits my hair, pulling my scalp, as Kelly shouts: 'Can you stop feeling sorry for yourself long enough to realize that other people have problems too?'

'Zeyneb!' Another voice, a familiar one.

I force open my sticky eyes. Throbbing leg. Shivering. My father is kneeling next to me.

Is this real? Is it a dream? Is *Baba* a monster?

'No, please, Baba!' I yell, covering my eyes with my hands.

'Wake up, Zeyneb!'

'Just go away and let me sleep . . . please . . .' I beg.

'Look at you. What's happened to your leg?' There's panic in his voice.

I see him pull out his phone from his coat pocket. I want to stop him but I can't find the will to move. I close my eyes and listen to his voice:

'Güler, it's me. I've found her. Phone the ambulance.'

No! This is *not* happening. All I wanted was a say in my own life, to get away, to make them realize they were wrong . . . I try to pull myself up to say this, to move, and an arrow of pain shoots through my entire body and I can't . . . I feel myself . . . I'm not very . . . I drop back down.

'She's broken her leg and she has a fever,' he says into the phone.

Then *Baba* picks me up in his big, strong arms and presses me tightly against his chest. 'Come here, *kizim*. It's going to be all right.'

22

I'm sitting up in a hospital bed. I can't remember how I got here. My leg's been set in an open splint and they've offered me food but I'm only interested in sipping a bit of tea. They're going to let me go home after the doctor's been to check on me, but I wish they wouldn't. There's not a single cell in my body that wants to go home.

As long as I'm in here everyone's fussing over me, making sure I have everything I need, putting on the concerned-family act. When I get home it will be a different story, I know.

The story of being spotted at the funfair holding a boy's hand. The story of running away from home. The story of consequences. A story I don't even want to begin thinking about. The biggest shark-problem ever.

I keep my head turned towards the wall and only respond to my family's enquiries when I absolutely have to. I just don't know what to say. Elif leans against the windowsill, facing me. It looks as if she's going to burst into tears any second. *Babaanne* clutches a bunch of slender yellow tulips, the ones from our garden, the ones I showed Alex. She should put them in water or else they'll wilt, but I'm not going to tell her that. Hopefully she'll think about it soon enough. My father is on a chair against the wall. He hasn't said a word since I came to.

Anne straightens the white bedspread for about the tenth time. I can see she doesn't know what to do to make me feel better. She's wondering how much of this is her fault. She doesn't want her daughter lying in hospital. I kind of feel sorry for her, but I dismiss it right away. If they'd treated me better, if they'd listened, then none of this would've happened. It's all their fault.

'Would you like some new pyjamas?' she offers. 'Those pink ones won't fit over your leg.'

I shrug.

'Blue, Zeyneb? Would you like blue pyjamas?'

I say nothing.

From the corner of my eye, I see *Baba* pull himself upright in his chair. His voice, when he speaks, is calm and deep and everyone listens.

'Why don't you all go down to the cafeteria? I want to speak to my daughter.'

Here it comes. I'd groan if I could. In fact, I'd swear if I could. I'd shout, 'But *I* don't want to talk to *you*! It's much too late for talking now. Where were you with your talking when I needed it?'

But I don't. I just lie here while *Anne* and *Babaanne* and Elif stand up and prepare to leave the room. My

170

mum casts one last longing glance in my direction, as if this is the last time she'll ever see me in her entire life. *Baba* gets up and walks over to my bedside. He sits down in the chair *Babaanne*'s just vacated and lays his large brown hand on mine.

'What you did, Zeyneb, everything that's happened...' he starts with a heavy voice.

Suddenly I'm all welled up with emotion. All sorts of emotion.

I'm grateful to him for finding me. I know how hard it must've been to look for me everywhere, to worry like that.

I'm relieved to see how much my parents love me, despite what they think I've done.

But I'm still angry. The same anger that made me jump out of my window last night. Angry at not being heard.

'No, wait, *Baba*. Let me speak. For once, please listen to me!'

He nods. He waits.

'I don't care what Semra told *Teyze* and what they told you and *Anne*. I didn't do anything wrong with Alex at the funfair.' The words are tripping over themselves in my rush to get them out. 'I know I'm not supposed to have a boyfriend, *Baba*, but he never was my boyfriend. I didn't disobey you in that, but I'd be lying if I said I never felt anything for him. I did . . . But that's just the thing. Feeling that way about a boy and *not* doing anything, that's the hard part, the part you have to be strong for. Not doing anything wrong because you're not interested in boys, that's easy. Anyone can do that. Didn't you ever like a girl before you met *Anne*?'

While I'm talking he's nodding his head. Either he's really listening to me or he's just pretending. I can't tell.

Then it's his turn to speak. Leaning forward, he puts his elbows on his thighs and holds his hands together in front of his face. 'Sometimes we're so occupied with how much *we* know, we forget that we can still learn from the young. I believe you when you say you didn't do anything with this boy, what's his name? Alex? I went to his house when I was looking for you and I learned that he is not a bad boy, this one.'

'No, Baba, you didn't!' He went to Alex's house . . . Oh, now I really do want to die.

'I thought you'd gone to his house. I phoned around for the address of this boy. You are my daughter, Zeyneb. You were gone. I had to find you. I had to look at the boy's house.'

'But, Baba, do you really think I would—'

'He was worried about you, this boy, his parents were worried. I wasn't pleased that I didn't find you, but I was pleased that I did not find you *there*.'

'How can you have so little faith in me? You've raised me well, with respect for my family and for my culture, how could . . .'

Baba stretches out one hand to touch the white bedspread covering my knees. 'I doubted myself as a parent. I wasn't sure if I'd guided you well enough. If maybe you'd got lost . . .'

'If you'd just bothered talking to me, I could've told you.'

'Yes, and that was my mistake. Not talking to you. But I spoke to the boy and he told me what you said: how being a good Muslim girl was more important than the feelings you had for him. He reminded me how much you love plants and told me you wanted to learn about this at university. That's when I thought of looking for you at the allotment. I am ashamed that I had to listen to a boy I don't know telling me all of this and that I couldn't listen to you.'

'Did you tell *Babaanne* everything when you were a boy?'

He's nodding. '*Babaanne* was less obsessed with the task of leading the young than I am. She's always known that sometimes they can lead us – *have* to lead us, in fact – or we'll stay stuck in the old ways for ever. Of course, they're not all wrong, the old ways, and we can't change everything in one go, but little by little we have to move into the future. And we're not the ones who are going to do that, Zeyneb. It's not my generation, it's yours. People like you who look at the world differently. I learned my way of looking at the world in Turkey. No, *kizim*, it's people like you who know what it's like to live here, who understand both cultures, who will lead us into the future, and that's . . . that's a very hard thing . . . for an old man like me to learn.'

Of course, I'm crying by now. 'But that's not what I want, *Baba*. That's not what I'm saying. I'm not a leader. I just want you to have faith in me. Not think you know everything before you've spoken to me. Not—'

'Ah, but that's where you're wrong, Zeyneb. You *are* a leader. Or you will be, some day. You'll be a professor of Botany and you'll discover new species of plants that you can name after me, your old, misguided father.' He smiles.

'I'm sorry, *Baba*. I'm sorry that I ran away and made you and *Anne* worry,' I sob.

'We are both sorry, it seems. But what have I told you about being sorry? It doesn't have to be a bad thing as long as . . .'

Through my tears I manage to smile, because I know what's coming. I've heard this line since I was a little girl. He's smiling too. We say it together: 'As long as you learn something from it.'

My father leans over and kisses me on the cheek. I feel like his daughter again. But at the same time I feel like his equal. It feels good.

23

'Zeyne-e-e-b!'

Just three more pages to go. Can't she wait till I've finished the book?

'Zeyne-e-e-b!'

It's an inborn gift, I swear. Knowing precisely, to the second, the most inconvenient time to call me. If it was an Olympic sport, my mum would win gold every four years.

I'm on my tummy under the hydrangea bush in the garden. The sun, where it breaks through the gaps in the leaves, bakes down on my bare arms. In front of me, crawling over a leaf, are two ladybirds, orange with black spots, and I've spent almost as much time watching them gobble aphids as I have reading *Pride and Prejudice*. I have a book review to hand in on Monday.

'Zeyne-e-e-b!'

'I'm coming, *Anne*,' I yell and crawl out from under the bush. Pulling myself up with my crutch, I start hobbling over to the back porch.

My plaster cast is covered in the names of the kids in my class. It was *Baba*'s suggestion, actually. The night before I went back to school he handed me a black marker. 'Can you still remember, when you were a little girl, how jealous you were when Elif broke her arm and her friends wrote all over her cast? Now it's your turn. You can ask everyone to sign yours.'

I grinned at him. 'Won't you sign first, *Baba*?'

Fumbling with the lid, he dropped the marker on the floor. I'd made him self-conscious. I picked it up and handed it to him. Carefully he wrote: *Ismet*.

'You should also ask the boy,' he said. 'What's his name again?'

'Alex,' I answered shyly.

'Yes, Alex. Let him sign too. Let all your friends sign.'

'Thanks, Baba, I will.'

And now it's there. *Alex*, it says in that confident handwriting of his. Right next to *Celeste* and *Jamal* and *Nicole*. Even Mr Rubens signed. All my friends, just like *Baba* said.

Now I see my mum's not alone at the back door.

'Where were you?' Kelly demands. 'I've been trying to get hold of you for the last hour.'

I come to a standstill in front of them and immediately my mum's hand shoots out to start picking grass off my T-shirt, muttering something under her breath. I try pushing her hand away, but she keeps at it.

'Trying to finish the book,' I answer and hold up my copy as proof. 'Have you read it?'

Kelly shrugs. 'I'll watch the film tonight. Listen, you want to go to the cinema? My mum's outside in the car. She can give us a lift.'

'Can I, *Anne*?' I look at my mum.

'Weren't you going to help me with the ironing?' she asks.

'Pleeease, *Anne*? I'll do it tonight. I promise.'

'But Zeyneb . . .' she starts, and I can see she's thought of another objection.

I drop my head to look down at my toes poking out of my cast. I know she's not going to let me go. But then I feel her hand under my chin. She tilts my face up until I'm looking into her eyes. She smiles. 'All right, go. Have you had anything to eat yet?'

In the dining room, draped over one of the chairs, is the thin cardigan I wear to cover my arms when I go out. I pull it on and do the buttons up.

'*Anne*?' I call. 'Where's—'

'In the drawer in the sideboard,' my mum calls back from the kitchen. 'You're old enough, Zeyneb, I shouldn't be tidying up after you.'

Rolling my eyes, I take the beautiful light blue fabric out of the drawer, pop a couple of hairpins between my lips and hobble over to the big mirror. Using the technique I found on the Internet, I wrap the headscarf around my new haircut. It's taken some getting used to but now I like it. I think I'll keep it like this for a while. I slide the hairpins over the headscarf to keep it in place and stare at the girl in the mirror. Olive skin, big brown eyes, high cheekbones, no hair visible under the tight, modern folds.

For three weeks it's been this girl staring back at me. This girl who's decided that wearing a headscarf, right now, at this point in her life, is the right thing to do. This is who I am. A good Muslim girl who wants to show her faith. Who I'll be later on, no one knows. Least of all me. A botanist? Maybe. A good Muslim woman. Yes, definitely that. A headscarf-wearing Muslim? I don't know. Depends if I come across any goats along the way who want to gobble up my lovely blue headscarf. What I do know is that I'll probably be able to handle it. I'm pretty sure I'm the same kind of gazelle as *Babaanne*.

Each time I look in the mirror, if I stare long enough, I see I'm not alone. Behind me are a whole bunch of other faces. It's not like I'm having hallucinations or anything – not like in *Baba*'s shed. I kind of conjure them up on purpose. To remind myself I'm not alone. To remind myself that these people help me to be me. I see Kelly. I see Elif. *Babaanne*. Mr Rubens is there too. And so are *Baba* and *Anne*.

I also see Zehra, the woman from the university, and I hear her voice: 'Do you have what it takes to spend half your time in your own culture and the other half in another culture without losing sight of who you are?'

I nod at the girl in the mirror. Yes, I think so. It's not easy, but I've done something difficult already and I know I can do it.

Kelly's at the door. 'Come on, Zeyneb, we're going to be late.' She smiles at my reflection.

'OK! I'm coming.' I smile back at her in the mirror. 'Dork!'

Many thanks to Sarah Scott for her invaluable help with this book. Also, the Brussels Writers' Group for all their years of support. Thank you.